9

DO YOU
LOVE YOUR
MOM
and Her Two-Hit
Multi-Target
Attacks
?

Dachima Inaka

Illustration by **Iida Pochi.**

"Right, everyone. We're ready to help!"

WISE
A high school Sage who doesn't have many good Christmas memories.

"If you consider how the children receiving the presents feel, these outfits are much more appropriate."

"I like being Santa!"

PORTA
A Traveling Merchant who's so pure that she still believes in Santa.

MEDHI
A high school Cleric with a surprising history of lovely Christmases.

MASATO OOSUKI GROWTH RECORD

Masato's Age: 0   I will never forget this moment. Thank you for being born.

Masato's Age: 1   First time pulling himself upright! His first steps! So many firsts.

Masato's Age: 2   His terrible twos—proof that he's growing. So many hugs from Mommy.

Masato's Age: 3   He's eating and growing so fast. Mommy's gotta cook more!

Masato's Age: 4   Kindergarten! Make lots of friends. And don't forget Mommy!

Masato's Age: 5   He learned to write and sent Mommy so many letters. Lifelong treasures.

Masato's Age: 6   Plays with friends more now. That's good. I know it is. *Sniff*

Masato's Age: 7   Elementary school! Ma-kun and Mommy can't wait for report cards!

Masato's Age: 8   A bit cheekier now, but still Mommy's little boy.

Masato's Age: 9   There's lots on his mind. Mommy will help think things through!

Masato's Age: 10   Officially a tween. I hope he gets through it all right.
I'll heap on the praise!

Masato's Age: 11   He's keeping more and more secrets… I guess this is just a phase…

Masato's Age: 12   So much naughty language! Mommy's gotta hang in there!

Masato's Age: 13   Junior high! I'm so glad he at least let us take a picture together!

Masato's Age: 14   We talk less, but he sure does eat more. That's healthy!
Everything's going to be okay.

Masato's Age: 15   Lots of stress about high school entrance exams. All I can do is watch.
Everything's going to be okay.

Masato's Age: 16   On an adventure with Ma-kun inside a game world! Every day is bliss.

"As requested by readers, here's Ma-kun's Growth Record!"

One day, Masato's party received a letter. It was from the editors of the all-mom magazine, *Maman*.

In fact, there were two letters. One was an invitation to the Mamademy Awards sponsored by that same publication.

The second was a cryptic message saying only "We expect great things from your hero son."

Despite confusion, the party got dressed up and went to the venue for the awards ceremony.

"What do they mean by 'great things'? Is something, like, bad gonna happen?"

"Beats me. But I think we can assume Mom has the award in the bag."

"Goodness, I'm not so sure about that. There are so many lovely mothers here!"

There were certainly a lot of beautifully dressed moms in the hall. Flawless makeup. The scent of their perfume wafting each time they stretched.

"The mommies have started doing warm-ups! They're ready for anything!"

"First comes the award. I wonder who will win it... Ah, it's starting."

The lights went out, and a drumroll echoed through the hall.

The master of ceremonies took the stage

and opened the envelope. He nodded as if the contents made perfect sense and then grabbed the microphone.

"The winner of this year's Best Maman Award is...Mamako Oosuki! Come on up here!"

"Oh my!"

A spotlight found Mamako. She seemed surprised by the thunderous applause. Wise and Medhi pushed her toward the stage.

Mamako accepted her award, and then it was time for her speech.

"My goodness! I don't know what to say. I'm so touched by all this! I'm at a loss for words... Oh, right! The letter said you were expecting great things from my son. Well, let me tell you all about Ma-kun, then."

"Huh?"

Masato felt like things were taking a dire turn.

He glared up at Mamako, but she came running over and grabbed his hand.

"No, wait! Mom?!"

"Ma-kun here cried so much when he was born! 'Such a healthy boy!' the midwife said. I was so happy!"

"Yeah, okay, that's enough! Stop, please! They're expecting things *from* me, not stories *about* me! Right?!"

Mom of the Year Award Revealed!

He glanced offstage, but the emcee simply gave him a thumbs-up, suggesting this was exactly what they'd planned. "So you're to blame?!"

"Now, now."

"Calm down." Wise and Medhi each pinned one of his arms, and Masato was unable to attack.

There were few things mothers loved talking about more than their children. The rest of the mothers in attendance were reminded of when their own children were young. No longer upset over losing the top award, they started nodding and clapping, listening happily to Mamako's speech.

"Ma-kun was such an active baby and always drank so much milk. I thought he was going to drain Mommy dry! Tee-hee!"

"I realize that's a natural thing for moms to talk about, but please, stopppp!"

But Masato's cries were in vain, and the speech went on far longer than originally planned.

MAMAN

EXCLUSIVE

CONTENTS

Dachima Inaka

Do You LOVE YOUR **MOM** and Her Two-Hit Multi-Target Attacks?

VOLUME 9

DACHIMA INAKA

Illustration by **IIDA POCHI.**

YEN ON

New York

Do You Love Your Mom and Her Two-Hit Multi-Target Attacks?, Vol. 9

▶ Dachima Inaka

▶ Translation by Andrew Cunningham

▶ Cover art by Iida Pochi.

TSUJO KOGEKI GA ZENTAI KOGEKI DE 2KAI KOGEKI NO OKASAN WA SUKI DESUKA? Vol. 9
©Dachima Inaka, Iida Pochi. (2019)
First published in Japan in 2019 by KADOKAWA CORPORATION, Tokyo.
English translation rights arranged with KADOKAWA CORPORATION, Tokyo,
through TUTTLE-MORI AGENCY, INC., Tokyo.

English translation © 2021 by Yen Press, LLC

First Yen On Edition: May 2021

Yen On is an imprint of Yen Press, LLC.
The Yen On name and logo are trademarks of Yen Press, LLC.

The publisher is not responsible for websites (or their content) that are not owned by the publisher.

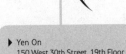

▶ Yen On
150 West 30th Street, 19th Floor
New York, NY 10001

▶ Visit us at yenpress.com
facebook.com/yenpress
twitter.com/yenpress
yenpress.tumblr.com
instagram.com/yenpress

Library of Congress Cataloging-in-Publication Data
Names: Inaka, Dachima, author. | Pochi, Iida, illustrator. |
    Cunningham, Andrew, 1979– translator.
Title: Do you love your mom and her two-hit multi-target attacks? /
    Dachima Inaka ; illustration by Iida Pochi. ; translation by
    Andrew Cunningham.
Other titles: Tsujo kogeki ga zentai kogeki de 2kai kogeki no
    okasan wa suki desuka?. English
Description: First Yen On edition. | New York : Yen On, 2018–
Identifiers: LCCN 2018030739 | ISBN 9781975328009 (v. 1 : pbk.) |
    ISBN 9781975328375 (v. 2 : pbk.) | ISBN 9781975328399 (v. 3 : pbk.) |
    ISBN 9781975328412 (v. 4 : pbk.) | ISBN 9781975359423 (v. 5 : pbk.) |
    ISBN 9781975359430 (v. 6 : pbk.) | ISBN 9781975306311 (v. 7 : pbk.) |
    ISBN 9781975306328 (v. 8 : pbk.) | ISBN 9781975318413 (v. 9 : pbk.)
Subjects: LCSH: Virtual reality—Fiction.
Classification: LCC PL871.5.N35 T7813 2018 | DDC 895.63/6—dc23
LC record available at https://lccn.loc.gov/2018030739

ISBNs: 978-1-9753-1841-3 (paperback)
       978-1-9753-1842-0 (ebook)

10 9 8 7 6 5 4 3 2 1

LSC-C

Printed in the United States of America

Prologue   The Heavenly Kings' Decree

Families came to the game to strengthen their bonds, but for many, it sowed the seeds of discord.

Such discord led to the rise of the Libere Rebellion. Their scheme placed the entire world in peril—but with the defeat of their ringleader, Dark-Mom Deathmother (aka Porta's mom, Saori Hotta), the matter should have been settled.

And yet.

"As those who struggle against maternal tyranny, we challenge you to a final battle!"

Their decree echoed across the road outside the Mom Shop, in the capital of Catharn.

Peering through the windows of the Mom Shop, Mamako, Wise the Sage, Medhi the Cleric, and Porta the Traveling Merchant were all struck speechless. Mone, Saori, and even Shiraaase all looked surprised.

There was one further witness—Hahako, peering around the corner of a nearby building, clutching her hands to her chest with worry.

Before them stood the remaining members of the Rebellion—Anti-Mom Amante, Scorn-Mom Sorella, and Frighten-Mom Fratello. Three of the Rebellion's Four Heavenly Kings, they had lost everything with the Rebellion's collapse. Possessed of the desperation afforded only to those with nothing to lose, they faced down the Hero, Masato.

"...You've gotta be kidding," Masato said.

"Oh, please. Do we have to explain every little thing?"

"After all thiiiiis, you should know we never joooooke. We mean iiiiit."

"Sonny, we ain't about to live down the things we done. We're stickin' to our guns like real men, never waverin', never yieldin'. To the bitter end."

"The bitter end? But—"

"Hold on! Back that up, dummies," Wise yelled, bursting out of the Mom Shop. She stopped next to Masato and looked over the three Kings with a mocking grin. "This whole grimdark tone isn't your thing! Don't be stupid. Just apologize! We'll happily chalk all the trouble you've caused up to role playing."

"Sheesh. Wise the 'Sage'! You appear to be *so stupid*, you're incapable of understanding human speech."

"Wha—? *Who's* the dumb one here?!"

"We would never apologiiiiiize."

"We came to settle things, ya hear? 'Cause I ain't gonna say it again. 'Sorry' ain't gonna cut it anyhow. Not after all we did…"

Porta and Medhi came running out, too.

"I was really mad before, but I'm not mad now! After all the trouble you caused, I finally got close with my mommy! That's more than enough for me!"

"A calm follows a storm. That's all that matters…but you're all far too stubborn to listen, aren't you? I brought a deterrent with me—one who can put an end to this foolish conflict."

Medhi turned to the ultimate deterrent: Mamako.

The Libere Kings were powerful foes. But they had lost their unique skills. They no longer had any means of defeating Mamako. She was the party's best defense.

Mamako glanced at Masato, checking if it was all right for her to hog the limelight here. Families didn't need words. Masato simply nodded back.

Mamako turned the nicest smile imaginable toward the three Kings.

"I think it's best we all take a deep breath and talk this over. We have some lovely tea and cake inside. Won't you join us?"

"Ha! I'm not dumb enough to go to war on an empty stomach! I'm so stuffed, I couldn't eat another bite!" *Growl.*

"Tea and caaaaake? Noooot iiiinterested." *Growl.*

"I ain't about to eat no sweet-tasting cake. I'm a real man." *Growl.*

"Oh my! You're even more stubborn than usual. Whatever should I do?"

Mone and Shiraaase were now standing in the window with a huge pile of cakes, making a big show of eating them. But the Kings stood firm.

"Just to be clear, we're not waging war out of frustration over being homeless, unemployed, and starving. This is our core belief!"

Amante drew the rapier from her hip. Her eyes were clear and burning with rage. She stared down at her needlelike blade.

"We're drawing a line in the saaaaand. Fighting moms is our thiiiing. If we didn't do thaaat, we couldn't be ourseeeelves."

Her eyes bewitchingly bleary, her smile clear as the sun, Sorella raised both hands. A tatami-sized magic tome appeared above her, the pages opening of their own accord.

"I'm gonna live my life however I want."

Fratello braced herself, a fire sparking in those dazed-looking eyes. The fighter claws hidden beneath her long sleeves glinted.

The three Kings meant business. This was intense. They felt like truly worthy foes.

"I don't know why you're being so hotheaded. Please, just—"

"Mom, that's enough. Respect your opponent's dignity. I think we've gotta do things their way here. All the battles we've had, it's natural to want to settle things properly."

"Masato Oosuki...I thank you. I'm glad you were my enemy. Admittedly not an enemy I was ever that concerned about, but—"

"You really don't need to make that point every time."

Amante smiled faintly, but only for an instant.

"Right, first, defensive walls on the buildings, don't want to damage anyone during the fight."

"You got it! ...*Spara la magia per mirare... Barriera!* And! *Barriera!*"

"A natural concern. *Spara la magia per mirare... Alto Barriera!*"

Wise and Medhi's spells activated, putting up a powerful defensive wall around them, protecting buildings and passersby from physical and magic attacks.

The party mages were definitely leveling up.

"Masato! I made this attack-boost drink! Here!"

"The perfect buff for me! Thanks, Porta!"

Masato took the medicine bottle from Porta and chugged it.

He then drew Firmamento and raised it to the sky. He swung it lightly, not intending to put any force behind it—but the shock wave it unleashed was so powerful, it sliced the clouds in twain.

Masato was hella buffed.

"Not bad! Okay, Mom, let's do this. For them."

"Yes, I suppose it's important to respect their feelings."

"Yep. We're ready. We can go all out."

"Okay then. Mommy will do her best, too!"

Mamako took a deep breath, and her smile faded. Her hands grasped the hilts of her Holy Swords. Terra di Madre, the Holy Sword of the Earth, and Altura, the Holy Sword of the Ocean, called on the divine will of mothers respecting their children's wishes, glittering with power.

The hero's party had lived through one tough adventure after another, and now they were about to show what they could *really* do.

The Libere Kings weren't scared or anything like that; no, they were just blinking a bit, like, slightly startled.

"G-good, you're finally ready! Great! Let's battle!"

"Let's go all ooooout! Get theeeeem!"

"Settle this in a single blow."

Blade against blade. Their eyes locked, sparks flying—and those sparks lit the fuse.

It was almost comforting. Like battles against storied rivals should be. This was the end, and Masato felt a tinge of sorrow. But it soon passed.

"Amante! Sorella! Fratello! It ends here! Come on!"

At his howl, the final battle began…

Chapter 1 A Fierce Battle Cry of Cock-a-Doodle-Doo... Huh? Why a Rooster?

Masato was surrounded by darkness. It felt like he'd woken up too early.

"Mm? Uh..."

He tried turning right, but bumped into a black wall.

He tried turning left and bumped into another.

"Kinda cramped... Oh, okay. I get it."

Masato lay on his back again and raised his hands upward.

Pushing against the darkness above—against the lid. As it opened, light and the sound of birdsong poured in. It *was* morning.

Masato sat up, and the coffin dissolved.

"I'm amazed I can sleep that well in a coffin...but that's not really something I should celebrate," he grumbled, taking in his surroundings.

This was a room at their inn in Catharn. The same type they always used, minimal furnishings, two beds.

Someone had flung the windows wide open, and the light streaming in was blinding. He was forced to shield his eyes with the sleeve of his pajamas.

He looked at the other bed and saw a girl lying there. Her pajama top had rolled up, leaving her belly button on display.

"Mmm...sonny, let's fight...mah..."

It was Fratello.

On the other bed was a woman in a skimpy negligee, sitting up with her chin on one hand, directing an alluring gaze his way.

"Good moooorning, Masatooo. Did you sleep weeeell?"

It was Sorella.

Fratello rolled over in her sleep. Masato looked at her, then up at Sorella, who waved.

He sighed.

"Whaaaat? You feeling siiiick?"

"No, nothing like that, just…"

"Spells work differently, depending on the caaaaster. We do need you dyyyying for the safety of us giiiiirls, but…perhaps it would be best if Wiiiise cast the death spell? Would you sleep better that waaaay?"

"I've long since accepted that death is what allows mixed-gender bedrooms, and frankly one coffin's the same as any other. That's not the problem…"

"Then I need to wake Fratello uuuup and chaaaange, so could you leeeeave?"

"You're just gonna ignore me then."

"Masatoooo, you can change in Mamako's rooooom. I'm sure it's empty by noooow. Go ooooon! Get ouuuut! You peeeerv!"

"I'm not a perv. But fine, fine, I'm going, geez."

Grumbling, he grabbed his gear and left the room. Masato is such a gentleman.

"Look, I've got good manners. I'll leave the room so they can change. That's not the problem. That's not what matters here."

Masato finished changing and tossed his pajamas in the laundry basket as if trying to discard his disgruntled feelings along with them.

He headed for the dining room. From the hall he could hear the sounds of breakfast being prepared.

Tap, tap, tap. Another tap, tap, tap. And one more tap, tap, tap. Three knives striking boards.

"Mom's a given, so then Wise? I don't even want to consider Medhi as a possible cook, so…Porta? Or maybe Hahako? She's staying here, too. Mm, probably her."

He poked his head in the door, scanning the room. He found Porta first. She was setting the table, making sure every seat had chopsticks and a soy sauce vessel, going back and forth between the table and the china cabinet.

When Porta dashed around like this, the two mascots slung from her shoulder bag bounced around. Piita had been joined by another knit doll, twice the size—Piitamama. This one was a bit misshapen, but that was part of its charm.

And a lovely sign of the restored bond between mother and daughter.

"Porta's setting the table, so the cooks are…"

He glanced to the kitchen.

"Oh, is that Ma-kun? I knew it! Good morning, Ma-kun!"

Mamako looked up from the quick-pickled cucumbers she was slicing. Her son sensor had gone off, and she flashed her unchanging smile at him. As expected.

Next to her…

"You overslept yesterday, but you're up early today. Good for you, Masato."

Hahako turned around, momentarily abandoning the quick-pickled eggplant she'd been slicing. She smiled, clearly enjoying herself more than necessary. Also expected.

So.

"Masato Oosuki! So good of you to join us. We need you to act as the judge and see which of us has sliced the most evenly!"

The girl slicing the pickled daikon spun around with an aggressive grin—not Wise, or even Medhi.

Instead of her black Rebellion cloak, she had an apron tied around her shoulders like a cape, completely missing the point of aprons. It was Amante.

Masato had a headache already.

"Come, Masato Oosuki! Judge this contest! This is no mere breakfast prep, but a duel! Make it snappy!"

"Leave me out of your dumb duels. And…"

"The apron? Heh-heh. You don't get it, Masato Oosuki. This is all the rage among girls these days, the latest trend in apron fashion. Wise the Sage and Medhi the Cleric told me all about it. It is our little secret. My opinion of them both has improved greatly."

"They totally tricked you, so...I'll just apologize on their behalf. And come on already, let me—gah!"

Before he could get out what he'd been trying to say all morning, someone grabbed his collar, strangling him.

"I overslept a bit, but we're here in time! Come on, Amante! This is a women's duel!"

"You have no right to go up against Mamako and Hahako! Allow us to demonstrate."

Masato's attempted killers were two other girls, both wearing aprons in the usual location.

Wise and Medhi. They stormed into the kitchen, leaving Masato gasping in their wake. Facing Amante down with indomitable grins.

"You're *both* wearing your aprons wrong!" Amante chided the two of them. "Girls should be more sensitive to the latest trends. Did you forget what you said last night? How foolish can you be?"

"Ohhh, sorry, we made that up. Never thought you'd actually believe it!"

"You WHAT?! Th-that's not fair!"

"To fool your enemies, first fool your enemies. It's fundamental. But we don't have much time, so let's get this cooking contest underway. I will do my best—"

""No, you won't.""

Wise and Amante teamed up to gently push Medhi out of the kitchen.

Mamako, Hahako, Wise, and Amante finished up breakfast.

"Hahako, can you check on the flavor of the miso soup?"

"Certainly. My, that's good. Should be ready to add the tofu."

"Hey, Amante, could you *not* keep taking the lid off? You'll let the steam out!"

"I—I know that, obviously! I was just checking to see if the rice kernels were standing properly! Humph!"

The kitchen was a little cramped, so there were many accidental shoulder bumps, hip shoves, or grind attacks. Very lively.

"M-Medhi!" Porta squeaked, seeing Medhi's dark power seeping out again. "I can't do all this myself! Could you please help?"

"Why, certainly," Medhi replied. Then she drooped again, muttering, "Porta asked me to help, so I am... I'm not being shoved out of the way because I'd only cause a disaster... No, definitely not..."

As Porta tried to cheer her up, Sorella and Fratello rolled in, finally dressed, and helped set the table. "Morniiiing!" "We late?"

Eight women. Everywhere you looked, there was youth of all varieties—whether beautiful, cute, or pretty. And the smell of good food filled the air.

What a paradise! Faced with this bountiful harem...

"That's the problem, though... Why are we all just going along with this? Please, people, think this through..."

The lone male party member should have been feeling extremely smug about all this, but instead, he was out in the hall, clutching his knees.

Breakfast was ready.

On one side of the big table in the center of the cafeteria were Mamako, Masato, and Porta. Across from them were Hahako, Wise, and Medhi. At the small table by the window were Amante, Sorella, and Fratello.

As always, the meal was extremely Japanese. When they'd worked their way through it and were sipping green tea, Masato decided this was his opportunity.

"Right, everyone, listen up. Heavenly Kings, you too. This is important."

Amante immediately spun around to glare at him.

"Masato Oosuki! I, too, have something important to say. First."

"Wh-what? Oh, I get it, you're finally—"

"We were included in 'everyone,' but you then call us out specifically? What's that supposed to mean? Enough of your discriminatory treatment! You can't just ostracize people!"

"It's not discriminatory, it's a reasonable distinction! Fine, I'll spell it out for you! You're all being way too buddy-buddy! It doesn't even make sense! Stop it!"

His voice rose to a shout, but Amante just snorted.

"Is that what this is about? Don't be such a nitwit. We're sworn enemies! We could never be buddy-buddy. Say, Wise the Sage, could you pass the teapot?"

"Sure thing! ...Oh, it's empty."

"Oh myyy! Should I brew another pottt?"

"Don't worry! This teapot still has some in it! Here!"

"Mm, thanks, Porta. Ya want some, too, Medhi?"

"Why, how thoughtful. You have excellent manners, Fratello."

"Hey! Leave some for me! I asked first!"

Clearly a conversation between sworn enemies.

Masato was on the verge of hurling his mug at the floor.

"If it was just the three Kings, that would be one thing! But our party is just as bad! I mean, I get that we never really *hated* them or anything, but...we were still enemies! This isn't right! It makes no sense! It's wrong! We've gotta do the right thing here!"

"We *are* doing the right thing. Humph."

"No, no, no, we obviously aren't. Amante, let's be clear. Do you even remember *why* you showed up outside the shop?"

"Of course! To challenge you to a final battle!"

"Exactly! You came here to fight! You made a decree and everything! And just as we thought we were finally gonna throw down..."

"But for all we talked about fighting, we've lost our skills, so we were sort of hoping against hope that you'd be nice and try to resolve things diplomatically, then when you guys got all fired up, too, we just, like, freaked out and—don't make me explain this!"

"So that's why you called a time-out just as we were about to attack. Trembling like newborn fawns, both hands held up, stammering, 'S-s-stop!'"

"I have no idea what you're talking about. Humph."

Amante turned her back on him and took a noisy sip of tea. Like she had no intention of continuing this conversation.

For the sake of her dignity, perhaps it was best to forget the specifics of how their battle had been averted.

"*Sigh*...then, Sorella, what happened next? We agreed not to fight, right?"

"That's riiiight. We decided to retreeeeat."

"Except you didn't. You're still here!"

"Weeeeell, we thought about iiiiit...and we had nowhere to goooo."

"Sounds like a thing you oughta know without thinking about it."

This seemed like a reasonable statement to him, but Sorella looked hurt and turned her back. Sipping her tea. Refusing to discuss it further.

"Well, we were perfectly aware of that fact ourselves and, frankly, a bit worried about it..."

"Before we came cruisin' for a fight, we checked up on y'all. We knew full well you folks were sleepin' alone in an inn room built for two. Seein' as ya got extra beds, we figured y'all can afford to put us up. It's just bein' practical."

"Fratello, let's put aside the fact that we're enemies for a moment and focus on the math. If I'm staying alone in a room meant for two, that means there's only one extra bed. Why did you think three extra people wouldn't pose a problem? I'd like a practical explanation of that, please."

Masato smiled like an elementary school teacher, but Fratello just turned her back on him. End of conversation. Nothing Masato could do about it. God damn it.

Masato picked up his mug to hurl it at the floor.

"Ma-kun, deep breath."

Mamako plucked the innocent mug from his hand before it could shatter, whispering in his ear.

"Ma-kun, Mommy doesn't think this is a bad thing. Certainly, we have history, but isn't being friends with the three Four Kings actually a good thing?"

"Sure, and if they stop getting up to no good and causing problems for us and the world and everyone can live in peace, that's good, but..."

But could they just go on like this? He didn't think so.

Masato looked across the table, toward Hahako and their former enemies.

What do we do about that *conflict?*

Hahako had not said a word since their meal had started—because she was focused on a battle of her own.

She was doing everything she could to get closer to the three Kings, as they were candidates to be her children. But every time she tried shifting her chair toward them, Amante glared at her, fending off the advance. Hahako would shift her chair back. This dance had been playing on a loop the whole meal.

The Kings are resisting...but it doesn't feel like they're completely against the idea, either.

At first, their attitude had definitely been outright rejection. Beyond their aversion to mothers in general, she was clearly at the top of their shit list.

But here they were, all eating in the same room. The gulf between them had gone from seemingly infinite to...close enough to reach out and touch.

They're one step away. They just need a catalyst...

And then maybe parent-child bonds could appear. The possibility felt tangible.

None of the Libere Kings would ever admit it, but perhaps they were sticking to Masato's party in the hopes that this possibility would come to fruition. He hoped so anyway. The more he thought about it, the more he wanted to hope.

In which case...

"We've spent so much time messing with other families. Preserving this tenuous peace isn't a bad thing, but if there's a better way of handling the situation, I'd want to do that instead. Maybe that's a bit presumptuous of me, but...I guess I really am the kind of hero who works for parent-child relationships rather than the sake of the world. I'm as horrified as anyone."

"Tee-hee, don't be. It's lovely! Mommy approves!"

He glanced sideways and saw Mamako all fired up. When she got excited like this, she breathed heavily, causing way too much wobbling. Total eye poison.

He took a moment to recover, then checked the other direction, scanning the rest of his party. Wise gave a shrug that said, "Why not?" Medhi and Porta were both nodding, Medhi with grace, Porta with enthusiasm.

Good friends to have.

"Right, in that case...let's get specific. Anyone got any good ideas?"

He looked around. Porta was frowning, head tilted to one side. Clearly thinking very hard.

Meanwhile, Wise and Medhi both immediately looked away, avoiding his gaze. *Such* good friends.

"Then...Mom."

"Let's do our best! Yay!"

"Not that, like...more concrete suggestions, please."

Masato gave her an expectant look, and Mamako met it with a smile. A long smile. She just kept smiling.

"Yes," she said at last. "Ma-kun, I know you can—"

"Honestly, I got absolutely nothing."

The Libere Kings had attacked, decreed their final battle...and instead of fighting, were just freeloading.

And Masato's party had an idea of what their general approach should be...but were unable to think of any concrete steps to make that happen.

They'd been stuck like this for a week now.

Once breakfast was over, they headed to the place where family problems were solved—the Mom Shop.

It looked like a fancy café, and when you opened the door, a pleasant chime rang.

"Hello! Welcome to...?"

The Mom Shop was permanently manned by Mone, who came

rushing out from behind the counter with a cheery customer service smile. This look soon faded to a frosty scowl.

"The Libere Lunatics are still with you?"

"*So* sorry. Masato Oosuki *insists* we stay, so what choice do we have? Humph!"

"We caaaan't turn down a request."

"Mm. 'Specially not from sonny here."

"Quit lying!"

"Well, if your party is keeping an eye on them, I don't mind. Come on in."

Mone seemed to have gotten used to visits from members of the secret society that had shaken the world to its core. Her attitude was much more like a clerk dealing with customers who only stopped in because they had nothing better to do with their sad lives.

The three Kings seemed used to that, too.

"Dark God Mammone! Yesterday you ran out of tea—have you resupplied?"

"Did that first thing this morning. It's on the shelf there, so help yourself. And quit calling me that! How many times do I have to tell you?"

Amante was already behind the counter making tea.

"Sooooo…let's all play pooooker. Wiiiiise! Medhiiiii! Ready to pay uuup?"

"I'm not letting you get a single mum today! I'm winning back everything you pilfered…everything you're holding for me! No cheating!"

"Don't worry, I've asked Porta to keep an eye on her. If there's anything strange, she'll—"

"Ah! Medhi, there's a card up your slee—mmph?"

"Porta, hush your mouth." Medhi smiled.

Sorella took over one corner of the counter, opening her gambler's area. Wise and Medhi were her main customers—the latter busy pinching Porta's lips shut. Wish them luck.

Nearby, Fratello was grunting as she worked out. She could now do five whole push-ups. Then she checked her muscles. They were coming along nicely!

They'd been here only a few minutes…

Masato let out a long sigh.

"They all just make themselves at home."

"It's far better than them making trouble, right? As for me…*rubrub!*"

"Augh, Mone! No surprise hugs! I mean, I get that it's necessary, but try and minimize the time spent rubbing your face on me."

"She has to be spoiled regularly, or her power will run amuck! *Rubrub.*"

"If that thirst isn't quenched, the consequences will be dire! *Rubrub.*"

"Mom, Hahako, there's no need for me to spoil either of you!"

Pushing back the opportunistic nuzzlers, Masato took a seat, and the other three joined him.

Mone was next to him, plastered to his side, and Mamako and Hahako were seated opposite him, smiling at the two of them—a situation that was definitely putting Masato's mind through the wringer.

Amante came stomping over. Without a word, she put four teacups and cakes down in front of them, and then stomped away.

"…Not the best manners, but not long ago I would never have imagined Amante serving Mom anything."

"That's right. It seems her attitude toward mothers has improved a lot! I'm so glad. I think you may yet have some hope, Hahako."

"I'd love that, but…I'm not so sure."

Hahako picked up the tea that Amante had made and brought it to her lips, savoring the taste. "Lovely," she said with a beatific smile. The smile of a mother doting on her child.

"Feels like you're one step away. But somebody's gotta make the final move. You can't just wait for it. I mean, it's been a week already! Like, what are you doing?"

"Mone's right, but…we just can't think of a good approach. Do you have any ideas, Mone? I suppose that's one reason why we came to the shop."

"Handling the difficult relationship problems is *your* job, Masato.

You're the ones who have ideas. And we had this conversation yester-day, and the day before."

"I know…"

He had a gloomy feeling they were going to be doing this tomorrow and the day after, too.

"Don't worry! It'll all work out," Mamako said firmly. She smiled. And kept smiling.

Just like she had at breakfast.

"Uh, Mom, do you actually have a basis for that? Like, something that's already in action, or something you're just waiting for the cards to align on?"

"Tee-hee. Good question!" She smiled.

"Suspicious…"

His sonstincts told him something wasn't quite right. Masato focused his mind, feeling their psychic connection. It got him nowhere. But just as he was about to give up…

The chime on the door rang. Inside the doorframe stood a nun…

"Everyone, good morn—gahhh!"

"Is Moko here? Oh, right, we're in the game! I should call you Porta."

Their usual quest giver was flung aside with all the force of a car crash, revealing a woman in ordinary villager clothes and glasses.

This woman had once been permanently exhausted, torn between the twin stressors of work and child-rearing. But now she was looking around the shop with expectation and hope.

"Oh! Mommy! My mommy's here!"

"Yes, it's your mommy! My daughter! My adorable daughter! Let me give you a big hug! Let me savor your presence bodily!"

This was Porta's mom, Saori. Porta went dashing over to her, and Saori swept her into a hug for the ages.

A Mother's Light activated immediately. An explosion of joy that sent blinding light in all directions.

"Good morning! You look great! I'm so happy!" *Rubrub!*

"Yes! I'm doing great! Are you, Mommy?! I hope so!"

"Of course! I'm great, too! I couldn't wait to see you again, so I woke up before dawn and started doing crunches for no reason! That's how great I'm doing! Did you eat breakfast?" *Rubrubrubrub!*

"I did! Mama's cooking and Hahako's cooking and Amante's cooking were all really good!"

"Th-that's nice! Then I'll have to get just as good at cooking! Will you eat what I make you?" *Rubrubrubrubrubrub!*

"Yes! I want to eat your cooking, Mommy!"

"Great! I'll do my best!" *Rubrubrubrubrubrubrubrub!*

It was impossible to see anything through the light, but Saori was rubbing Porta's cheek! And rubbing her cheek on Porta's cheek! And rubbing Porta's head! And rubbing her cheek on Porta's head! Rubbing her everywhere rubbing could be done!

A touching reunion between a mother and a daughter parted by fate.

"...Um, Saori? I hate to interrupt, but—"

"Oh, Masato! Thanks for looking after my adorable daughter! Thank you for being so kind to her! What is it?"

"You're under arrest on suspicion of murder."

There was a single coffin lying in the entrance to the Mom Shop. With you-know-who inside.

Medhi cast a resurrection spell.

"Let us begin again! Good morning, everyone. As you're aware, I am Shiraaase. And though I need not infooorm you again, this is not Saori Hotta, but Dark-Mom Deathmother. Make sure you don't get that wrong."

"Shiraaase, please, forgive me... At least show some mercy with the outfit..."

"Don't worry, Mommy! Even if your account name is a bit strange, and your outfit is trying way too hard, you're still my mommy!"

"Thank you. But this is a shame I'd prefer to leave buried in my past. Having it dug up like this is making me want to cry."

Black armor. A Rebellion coat. Horns. Her name—Dark-Mom Deathmother.

A name worthy of a JRPG final boss—with an outfit to match.

Forced back into this form, Deathmother was sitting awkwardly on a chair. Frankly, this was a pretty mild punishment for murder, so she should count herself lucky.

Their guests were Shiraaase and Saori—er, Dark-Mom Death-mother. Porta was still plastered to the latter. On the other side of the table were Mamako, Hahako, and Mone.

"With introductions complete, allow me to infooorm you of the reason for our visit."

"Please do, Shiraaase. What brings you and Deathmother here? Good news?"

"Even Mamako's calling me that...*sniff*..." Deathmother choked back a sob. "But you're right. Our preparations are complete. We just have the final checks."

"Which means...are you three ready to serve as padding?" asked Shiraaase.

"What are we, cushions? Whatever."

Masato, Wise, and Medhi were seated at the counter.

The three ex–Libere members were behind it, looking glum. Hackles raised, keeping as far from their former boss, Dark-Mom Death-mother, as they could.

"It's our job to keep the three Four Kings from doing anything stupid? Got it."

"Well then."

Shiraaase looked back at Deathmother and nodded.

"Amante, Sorella, Fratello. Today I can infooorm you...no, *inform* you of something very important."

"Huh...? No extended *o*'s? You're Shiraaase, but just 'informing' like normal? No way!"

"Oh deeear! Shiraaase isn't gooooofing around! This is gonna be, like, seriooooous!"

"Mm...I'm trembling with anticipation! Like a warrior!" Fratello was shaking like a leaf.

"Correct. This is of the utmost importance. Listen carefully."

For once, even Shiraaase looked tense.

*   *   *

"Management has officially approved your designation as a family: Hahako as your mother and, in order of age, Sorella as the eldest daughter, Amante as the second daughter, and Fratello as the third daughter."

A silence fell. Mamako started clapping, and Mone soon joined her. Their applause echoed through the room.

Hahako clapped both hands over her mouth, stunned.

The three Kings were staring wide-eyed, mouths agape, frozen to the spot.

"Oh? Surprising. I expected vehement resistance. Perhaps things will work out after all. Families forever!"

"Th-that's not true at all! We're vehement! Just...Masato Oosuki!"

"Ow!"

Amante had smacked him upside the head. **Damage: 1.**

"Th-that's riiiight! We're resisting violentlyyyy! Wiiiise!"

"Ow! No, wait, that didn't actually hurt."

Sorella had slapped Wise. **Damage: 0.**

Fratello raised a hand to Medhi...

"What's that hand for?" She smiled.

"...Nothin'! Spare me the terrifyin' grin!"

Sensing danger, Fratello quickly turned. "She spooked you?" "She did not!" And punched Masato in the face. **Damage: 1.**

That was the extent of the Kings' resistance.

"I kinda figured this would happen. So are you feeling up to it? Are you at least a *little* curious?"

"I—I dunno about that! It's just...Hahako *did* save us, and maaaaybe I got to wondering what having a mom would be like, but I'm not going to explain that! Ha!"

"You just did, though. Not that it matters."

"As for me and Fratelloooooo, Medhi's mother treated our injuriiiiies, and that got us thinkiiiing. Stiiiilll...you can *call* use a familyyyy, but we don't really get iiiiit. We've never *had* parents befoooore. And never been anyone's childreeeeen."

"Er…then what?"

"Sonny, all we ever had was a desire to rebel against the dominion of parents. Never knew nothin' more. So nothin' doin'. See ya around."

"No, wait, where are you going?"

The three of them were ducking under Hahako's gaze, quickly moving to the door.

They stopped at the entrance, staring at the ground.

"If you want to make Hahako our mother, suit yourself. That's just an easy change in our files. Knock yourself out."

Amante's voice was half lonely, half apathetic. And with that, they left the Mom Shop.

Soon, their heads were visible in the window. They didn't go far. Masato decided that was a relief.

Wise and Medhi were both looking at him. Both thinking the same thing. But Masato didn't have an answer.

"…Shiraaase, can you inform us?"

"Very well."

"Wait, I'll do it. I'm the cause of everything, after all."

Dark-Mom Deathmother sat up and pushed Porta upright, too.

"Amante, Sorella, and Fratello are all NPCs. They were originally created as background adventurers, but the character designs were a bit too distinctive, to the point where they threatened to outshine the player characters, so they were never fully implemented."

"So they were originally scrapped? That's a brutal backstory."

"But going from that to the Four Kings is a huge promotion," noted Wise.

"It seemed a shame to just throw them out, so I was looking for another use. I originally meant to make them guards for my daughter, to go on adventures with her in my stead."

"Huh…that explains why they were never able to be mean to her. Parts of that code are still live."

"And there were always four rooms ready in every lair," said Medhi. "Were those originally...?"

"Exactly. I intended for them to be bases for my daughter's party. I had my subordinates secretly place them all over the world."

"Abuse of workplace authority, all in the name of parental affection."

"You're merciless, Medhi. But...also on the money," Dark-Mom Deathmother admitted, stroking Porta's head.

She'd done it all for her beloved daughter. That was both delightful and not quite cause for celebration. Even Porta wore a complicated expression, though she didn't try to escape the head rubs.

"But just before they were fully implemented, the stress got to me, and I changed my plans. Amante, Sorella, and Fratello were adjusted based on data from rebellious children and sent out to fight against the concept of a world made for family bonding. I did that to them. And I forced them to do my bidding."

"But everything ended well, and now they're trying to change. That's what 'all's well that ends well' means. Hee-hee."

Mamako looked as cheery as Dark-Mom Deathmother did gloomy. No gloom could stand against that smile.

Masato's entire party agreed with Mamako—it had ended well. They were all nodding.

"And now that the final checks are complete, let's discuss the future!"

"Yikes, way to shatter the mood! Why are you all fired up?"

Shiraaase had leaped to her feet—possibly frustrated by not being the one in charge of informing people. She turned to Hahako, who blinked at her.

"Hahako, let us begin by hearing your position. Do you have any objection to making the three Kings your children?"

"Of course not. I'd be glad to have them. But if we are simply rewriting their data and forcing them to be my children, then I'm afraid I must refuse."

"Don't worry about that. Management has simply decreed they are *allowed* to be your children. Nothing is decided yet."

"In other words, they're ready to make the change if we request it?"

"Exactly. Frankly, given your connection to the main system, Hahako, you can change the data yourself. You chose not to. No matter how much they rejected you, you persevered, patiently trying to connect with them. Reprogramming their minds would be easy, but it would be nothing but an insult to your feelings—to a mother's emotions. We would never do that."

"I see…thank you. I'm grateful for management's sound judgment."

"You're welcome. On the other hand, it does seem like this decision makes it more difficult for you to ever be family. That can only be achieved if Amante, Sorella, and Fratello change voluntarily. As for how we can encourage that…hmm."

Shiraaase made a show of pondering the matter and then turned to Masato. She raised a hand.

"Excuse me, can I place an order? The usual, please."

"Don't act like one of our regulars! But fine, I get it. You're just throwing the whole thing to us, like always."

"Management will be in charge of things this time," explained Deathmother. "We've got a lovely event in store for you. It's quite a pretty big deal, the kind of thing you only get going if a producer calls in a lot of favors. I basically bullied everyone into it. It was textbook power harassment, if I'm being honest."

"…Mommy…" *Sniff.*

"Moko?! I'm not a mean person, I promise! The schedule was just a *bit* tight, but all I did was ask my subordinates *nicely* if they could work a little harder!"

"But before I infooorm you of the details, we'd better convince the event's targets to participate."

The heads of the three Kings were still lined up right outside the window.

They were leaning against the exterior wall of the Mom Shop, doing nothing. Passersby were giving them funny looks, but they didn't care. All three girls were simply staring at their feet.

They must have noticed when Masato's party came outside.

"Where do they rewrite our data?" Amante asked. "Go on, take us there."

Her lips quivered. She didn't look up.

"Don't just give in like that, damn. What do you think?"

"Maybe we should try punching them? Yell 'Screw you!' and go in swinging like always?"

"Very well, Wise," said Medhi. "Please, rain attack spells down on your defenseless opponents in full view of the public eye."

"Phrasing! That's not what I meant… Fine, what *do* we do?"

"I could make some medicine to make them feel better!" offered Porta.

"Not the worst idea, but this problem is mental, not physical—not sure your medicines would do the trick. Which means…"

"This is Mommy's job! I have an idea," Mamako said, stepping forward.

But even faced with the ultimate mom, the Kings did not respond.

"Girls, a moment, please? Ready?"

Looking grave, Mamako put her hand on her hip and raised an index finger.

"Er…is that…n-n-no, wait a minute!"

"Eeeeeeeek! Why, whyyyyy? Is she gonna fire that thiiiing?"

"Good-bye, life…"

The Kings clutched each other, tears streaming, as Mamako prepared to unlock the ultimate move, the laser cannon of scolding!

Apparently.

"Let's call this our final battle!" Mamako said, smiling. She waggled her finger gently.

The three girls stared up at her, mouths agape. Then they scrambled to their feet.

"A final battle? Okay, fine. You don't need to explain that! We'll die in combat, like true warriors! And when we wake up, we'll be different people. Fine. Let's fight!"

"Wait, not like that. We're not fighting with swords and magic.

Instead—there's an event starting soon. Let's all join that event and settle things there."

"An eveeeeent? Whaaaat? What kind of eveeeent?"

"A special one, designed to allow parents and children to share their feelings and build wonderful memories together. You'll learn more once you join in."

"And how in the heck is that gonna settle it?"

"If the three of you accept your mother and decide to be her children, we win. If that doesn't happen, hmm…"

Mamako thought about it and then turned to her party.

What should they do if this didn't work? Masato, Wise, Medhi, and Porta all frowned, tilting their heads to one side. No ideas came.

"Um…Amante, what do you think?"

"Don't ask me! Figure it out yourselves! No need to do all this… beating around the bush! Just rewrite our data."

"I'm not letting them do that."

The wall of the building suddenly morphed outward, turning into Hahako.

"I don't want anyone but the three of you as my children. I want you as you are now. If it's a different version of you, it doesn't count."

Her feelings were palpable, and earnest.

Hahako's gaze and words landed direct hits on the girls, leaving them stunned—and then their faces turned red, and they all stared at the ground.

"Where did that come from…? Geez, you can't just—"

"I'm sorry to flummox you like that. But I meant every word. I'm serious about this. Will you please join us in this event?"

"Uuuumm, I thiiiink…if Amante's in, then I am, tooooo."

"Yeah, if y'all are in, then I might as well tag along."

"You're putting this all on me? Argh! Arghhhh!"

Amante stomped her foot a few times, at a loss. Then she thrust a finger out toward Hahako.

"Fine! We'll join this dumb event! On one condition!"

"And that is?"

"If we win this match, then *you* decide what to do with us! Don't force me to make any more decisions! Got it?!"

"Sounds like the worst possible use of a victory."

"It seems you've talked them into it!" Shiraaase said, sweeping out of the shop. "Let's get going."

Behind her was Dark-Mom Deathmother, hiding behind Mone so as to avoid antagonizing the three Four Kings.

"Get going? To where? Are you gonna explain this?"

"I figured it would be best if I dole out the infooormation a little at a time, tormenting you all. One, two, three…twelve of us in all. Quite a large party."

Mamako, Masato, Wise, Medhi, and Porta.

Hahako, Amante, Sorella, and Fratello.

Shiraaase, Dark-Mom Deathmother, and…

"Huh? Wait, me too?" Mone said, pointing at herself in surprise.

Shiraaase nodded. "It would never do to leave you out, would it? Why not join everyone this time?"

"I'm glad to be part of things, sure, but…honestly, I don't care about the Libere Kings."

"Ha-ha-ha! Perhaps a bit too honest." Shiraaase cackled.

"Rude!" "Ruuuude!" "Mm." All three Kings of the Libere Rebellion turned and smacked Masato. "Why me?!" He just happened to be standing closest to them.

"Well, regardless of your interest in them, our next destination is where the Dark God Mammone was originally going to be placed. What do you say, fancy a visit home?"

"Huh, really? I would like to check that out! Uh, but…"

"Don't concern yourself about the Mom Shop. I've called in a pinch hitter. She'll be here any moment…oh, there she is."

An extremely nondescript woman was coming down the street.

She waved when she saw Mone—this was Mone's mother, Leene.

"Oh, Mommy! You're gonna take over the shop?"

"I am. I heard all about it. Take a nice long look at the place where you were supposed to be."

"Thanks! Oh, but I promise I'll come back. I mean, I'm—"

"Of course, dear daughter. Dark God or not, you're my precious little Mone."

"Yeah! And you're my mommy! I love you!"

Mother and daughter embraced. "Mommy!" "You're so spoiled!" And Mone absorbed her dose of spoiling. Lots of nuzzling was involved. And so Mone's affection reserves were filled to the brim.

Amante watched this closely.

"...Masato Oosuki," she said. "Are they not *actually* mother and daughter?"

"Technically speaking, no. Mone is a Dark God, and her mother, Leene, is an ordinary person. Mone had nowhere to go, so Leene took her in. They didn't start out as mother and daughter. But they sure are now."

"Hmmmm... I seeeeee..."

"Ya don't even have to be related to be family, eh...? Well, I'll be damned..."

Sorella and Fratello were watching, too, eyes bleary and dazed, respectively.

There was no need to rush this journey. They had to work toward it, one step at a time, one impression and feeling after another.

Masato's party could wait until the three Kings were—"Oh, I feel dizzy..." "Mommy?!" Mone had absorbed too much, and Leene keeled over. The Kings' observation of family bonds in action came to an abrupt end.

The party set out. All twelve of them tromping along down the road out of Catharn, into the fields outside.

The monsters quivered in fear, the difference in strength clear, but, "Don't worry, we won't attack good children!" """"Squeee!"""" Mamako just pet them all.

They were headed to the transport point on the dais above. At the top of a long flight of stairs was a magical circle, surrounded by stone pillars.

"This will take us to the Transport Palace, and from there to a world on a different server?"

"We're not changing servers this time. Just using this facility to allow us to transfer to a unique location ordinary transport spells can't access. Deathmother, prepare the Key Items."

"We're sticking with that name, then? You're so persistent."

Dark-Mom Deathmother held up her hand. Above her head, a monstrous shoulder bag appeared out of thin air, its mouth yawning open. She pulled three items out of it.

The first was a small, lidless square box. The kind used to measure liquids and grains in traditional cooking. A *masu*.

Next, a small bottle. The label said, VINEGAR. *Su*.

Finally, something round and covered in spikes, like a sea urchin. It was actually a chestnut still in its burr. A *kuri*.

"For Key Items, these sure are rather mundane household objects..."

"Heroes! Hold aloft the Key Items, and summon the portal to the Forbidden Realm!"

"Fine, we'll do it," Wise grumbled. "But this is gonna make us look real stupid."

"I see that smirk, Amante," Medhi snapped. "We'll have words about this later."

Masato took the chestnut, Wise the vinegar, and Medhi the box. They held them aloft, wincing.

And a huge door appeared over the transport point. Bells rang, and the door slowly swung open.

Beyond the door was an unspoiled field of snow and trees covered in ice, glittering in the sun.

"This lies at the edge of the Catharn Kingdom. The highest mountain in the Motherest Mountains, Mount Motherest itself. Are you ready?"

"It's so beautiful!" Porta gasped. "And...whoa...it's so cold!"

"Don't worry, we've prepared warm clothes. Here."

The monster shoulder bag opened its maw once more. Out came winter coats, scarves, gloves, and earmuffs.

Dark-Mom Deathmother's primary occupation was Merchant. With the mom boosts, she possessed an infinite supply of any item. Nothing was left out. Masato's party were able to pick whatever winter gear they liked.

But the three Heavenly Kings just stood and watched, not trying to equip anything.

"Yo, what are you doing? Join in!" shouted Masato.

"We have our Rebellion coats. We're not cold!"

"Really? I mean, Sorella and Fratello are at least wearing their coats, but you've just got yours slung over your shoulders, Amante! At least put your arms through the sleeves."

"I said I'm not cold! Humph!"

Amante spun around and led the other two through the door. "Crap, that's...er, so not cold!" An icicle formed instantly at her nose, and she snapped it off and threw it away.

Dark-Mom Deathmother watched them trudge away, saying nothing.

"Geez, they're so stubborn...I'm gonna go yell at 'em."

"Wait, Masato," Deathmother said. "It's fine. It's not me they need to worry about now. Let them focus on their relationship with Hahako."

She'd created the Libere Kings and used them as she pleased.

This left a deep rift between them.

So they've got issues with the mother looking after them, and the one who created them...would be nice if we could resolve both.

But chasing after two rabbits would get you neither. It was probably best to focus on a single objective for now.

"If you say so, Deathmother. We'll do it your way."

"Thank you. But Masato, if you really wish to consider my feelings, please...stop calling me by that painful name."

"Deathmother, let's go," said Wise.

"Deathmother, watch your step, the snow is very deep," cautioned Medhi.

"Mommy Deathmother! Can I walk with you?"

"Hurry up, Deathmother, or we'll leave you behind!"

"I know you're not bad children, but why do you have to do this? ...Is someone setting a bad example...?"

"Deathmother, shall we proceed? I can infooorm you the rest of us are leaving."

"Aha. The root of all evil."

"Let's give this everything we've got, Deathmother! Yay!"

"Deathmother, if we don't hurry, we'll lose sight of the children. Come on!"

"You're trying to cheer me up because I seem depressed, is that it? I'm choosing to believe it is."

Tears streaming down her face, she stepped into the frozen world.

"Right, everyone! You know you wanna yell it, so let's go! One, two, three—"

"""""Snowwww!"""""

Snow, snow, snow! Gleaming white in all directions!

Masato scooped up some soft, white powder and balled it up. "Okay, Masato versus everyone!" "Who chose those teams?!" An all-out snowball fight broke out.

Then they struck strange poses, falling over in the snow, seeing who could leave the silliest imprint. "And then bury Masato Oosuki alive!" """""Yeah!""""" "Why?!" A Masato-shaped snowman was formed. Laughter rang out as the party forged onward...

After about half an hour of this, everyone got really tired.

The snow field seemed endless. It was very hard to walk through. Exhausting.

Masato glared up at the three Four Kings, who were riding on a giant magic tome, and sighed.

"...Shiraaase, how much farther?" he asked.

"Good question. It shouldn't be long now."

"We're not, like, lost, are we? 'Cause I'll be pissed if we are," said Wise.

"No need to fret. I can see the landmark ahead."

Shiraaase pointed. There was a pointy treetop in the distance, covered in ice. The way the sun hit it made it sparkle like holiday lights. It was lovely.

They could see it, but...no matter how far they walked, they still couldn't make out the whole tree. Even after thirty minutes.

And then...

"Wait a second...the clouds...the winds picking up...that's not a good sign..."

"Weather in these mountains can be fickle. In the blink of an eye, a blizz—"

BLIZZARD. Suddenly pounded by furious wind and snow, Shiraaase was instantly coffinized.

"Oh my! How awful! Everyone, gather close!"

"This calls for desperate measures! Use Shiraaase's coffin as a shield! Quick!"

"Eek! You don't have to be Shiraaase to die in this!"

Mamako and Hahako pulled out their respective Terra di Madres and tried erecting an earthen barrier, but the weight of the snow kept the ground where it was.

There was a thud nearby as the magic tome landed, the Libere Kings frozen stiff on the back of it. They were done for.

"An item to warm them...whoa! My bag is frozen! I can't open it!"

"Don't worry. Leave this to Mommy...huh? Mine, too?!"

Dark-Mom Deathmother's shoulder bag was blasted by the blizzard, turning into a giant snowball and falling to the ground.

Shiraaase's coffin, the magic tome with the three Kings frozen to it—with no better options, they lined these up, forming a barrier against the horizontal snow.

Huddled together and shivering, Masato's party was soon buried alive.

"Crap, crap, crap, cold, cold, crap, cold!"

"I know it's cold! Don't keep chanting it!"

"Wise, Mone, stay quiet. Very quiet...*zzz*..."

"Don't fall asleep, Medhi! Eyes open! Augh...my eyelids are so heavy..."

"We're in grave danger. My power will get us out of this! I was so close to having my wish granted...we'd come so far. It's a shame, but this is the only way!"

Hahako put her arms around the frozen Kings, and then white hands reached out from every inch of her body.

These hands wrapped themselves around everyone, pulling them down beneath the surface of the snow. Into the sea of data that made up the game world—a trick only Hahako could pull off.

But...

"Wait! Moments like these must be solved with parent-child bonds! Let us overcome this with the power of mothers!"

Mamako's voice rang out, every bit as loud as the howling blizzard winds.

Hahako slowly lifted her head, looking up at Mamako.

And so did the other mother. Porta was in her arms, falling asleep. Dark-Mom Deathmother slapped her own cheeks hard, looking grim.

"The power of mothers...yes! That's true! We're all mothers!"

"I have little experience as one, but this is exactly the time for me to grow as a mother! What mother could fail to protect her precious child?"

"That's the spirit! Come on, you two! There's only one thing to do here!"

Mamako, Hahako, Dark-Mom Deathmother—all three nodded.

And took off their clothes.

"What the—nooooo, don't warm us with your fleeeeesh!"

""""Huh? What's wrong with it?"""""

Masato forced his eyes open, sensing a threat to his sanctity.

He found himself face-to-face with three topless mothers, one his own. Skin as white as the driving snow, six round swellings—Dark-Mom Deathmother was every bit as gifted as the other two.

It was all very soft and warm. And warmth was exactly what he needed right now, but...

"Don't worry, Masato. I can't feel cold. I'm fine, even without my clothes."

"Maybe you're fine, Hahako, but that's not my concern here! Flesh contact is strictly prohib—oh crap, I'm getting sleepy again…"

"Ma-kun! Hang in there! Oh dear. If we can't warm him physically…oh, I know! Just like before!"

Mamako swiftly fixed her clothing and then took Masato's hand in hers.

Pat, pat, pat. Pat, pat, pat. She tapped out a gentle rhythm.

Uh…what the heck is she doing?

Completely baffled, Masato felt even more ready to pass out.

But then a memory came back to him, like his life passing before his eyes.

A winter's day. Masato was playing in a snowy area meant for kids.

He'd been busying himself alone, making a big snow pile, and his hands had turned all red.

"Mommyyy! My hands hurt! Wahhh!"

"Oh my! They've gotten so cold. I'll tell you what…"

Now and then, Mamako was permanently young. She put his hands in hers and went pat pat pat, pat pat pat, tapping them lightly.

"Sniff…Mommy, what are you doing?"

"I tap you six times—that's called *rokubute.* Do you know what that means? Can you say it backwards?"

The scene from his memories faded.

"…Huh? I'm all warm."

Masato's mind cleared. He wasn't cold anymore. Even his face felt normal. A second ago he'd been totally freezing, but…

A special mom skill. The name—**Rokubute Mom.**

To clarify, *Rokubute* means "six taps," but if you write it backward, you get *tebukuro*—the Japanese word for "gloves."

The gloves Mom had woven for him were *six* times warmer and protected Masato's entire body! They applied the Null Freeze status!

"So you developed another weird power...but it definitely helped. Thanks."

"I'm glad you're safe, Ma-kun. I'll have to do the same for Wise, Medhi, and Mone. The other children have their own mothers looking after them."

"That's right," agreed Hahako. "I, too, am a mother."

"I'm not too sure I can do it as well as Mamako, but as a mother, I have to try! I know one thing for sure—my love for my daughter is every bit as strong."

Dark-Mom Deathmother started patting Porta's hands. *Pat pat pat. Pat pat pat. Patpatpatpatpatpat*...it took eighteen pats before Porta's eyes finally opened. Success!

The other three were soon pulled from their dangerous slumber by Mamako's swift treatment. "Mm?" "Oh?" "Huh?" All safe and sound.

As for Hahako...

"I know I can do it. I'll prove I can."

She used Rokubute Mom on the frozen Kings. Her powerful desire to become a mother activated. Cracks appeared in the ice covering them—and the ice shattered.

Saved, the Libere Kings were eternally grateful, the distance between them—

"Hahako, let go of our hands! What are you doing?"

"Well, um...I'm not sure..."

"It was snoooowing...and we got sleeeepy...and that's the last thing I remembeeeer."

"Hahako did somethin'. Can't let yer guard down!"

"Hee-hee-hee. I'm sorry. But I'm glad you're all safe. That's all that matters."

Their obliviousness and Hahako's natural reserve had left things unchanged. How unfortunate.

Anyway...

The blizzard had stopped, and the skies had cleared. The snowfield was sparkling again.

Everyone but Shiraaase was safe and sound, so they set off once more.

"No telling when the weather's gonna turn again," said Masato. "We'd better hurry."

"No time to waste. Which means…"

"From here on, it's a gentle downslope. Let's make this quick—using this sled."

Medhi pointed at Shiraaase's coffin.

The lid opened slightly, and the lady inside reached out a hand to give them a thumbs-up.

"Seems she's on board, but…should we really?"

"If Shiraaase agrees, I don't see the issue. Porta, will you raise the coffin's maneuverability and handling so we can all sled in safety? Maybe get your mom to help."

"Yes! I want to work on this with Mommy!"

Dark-Mom Deathmother happily opened her shoulder bag, spying a chance to prove herself. She pulled out runners and a handle, and Porta quickly attached them to the coffin.

With the improvements made, the coffin sled was complete.

"The three Four Kings on the magic tome, and everyone else on the sled. Ready, Ma-kun?"

"So I'm steering, like the hero and party leader should? Maybe not a vehicle I can be proud to drive, but…"

Pushed by Wise's wind magic, the coffin sled started sliding. From the level ground to a gentle slope. Not too fast, not too slow, very smooth.

After a while, the area around them opened up. Ahead of them loomed a giant tree, far bigger than those around them, like a mountain made of wood.

"That's huge!" exclaimed Wise. "You could build a whole house from that one tree! What kind of tree is it?"

"I'll appraise it! Hnggg…oh, that's a fir tree!"

"A fir tree…," repeated Medhi. "Wait, is this event going to be…?"

"Yep, seems like it. Here we are!"

Masato turned the handles, angling the runners inward and slowing them down. The coffin sled slid to a smooth stop in front of the giant fir.

Time to get the details. Medhi cast a resurrection spell. The coffin vanished, and Shiraaase sat up.

Somehow she still had runners attached to her back, and handles on her head, but everyone pretended not to notice. If they didn't point it out, she'd never be the wiser.

"I agreed to serve as a sled, but I do not recall granting permission for these improvements! Saori Deathmother Hotta, we shall have words later."

"Now she's acting like it's my middle name…that's almost worse…"

It seemed she was the wiser after all. Moving on…

Shiraaase had them all gather before the giant fir.

"Nice work getting here in one piece. Allow me to infooorm you of your whereabouts. This is where the Saori Hotta Castle once stood."

"That would have been a *good* place to use the Deathmother moniker…"

"And that castle was where we'd originally intended Mammone the Dark God to live. Implementation got delayed, a certain producer took over the data, redid the whole shebang as a Rebellion lair, and used it for nefarious purposes, so sadly the entire set of assets was eliminated. Poor assets!"

"My home…" *Stare.*

"Mommy…" *Stare.*

"I'm so, so, so, so, so sorry…!"

Mone and Porta's forlorn stares quickly reduced Dark-Mom Deathmother's HP to 0.

Shiraaase tapped the trunk of the giant fir, getting their attention back on her.

"And that brings us to the main infooormation! This event will be—"

"Yeah, we know. Christmas! …Ah! Crap, that just slipped out!"

They'd used the chestnuts (*kuri*), vinegar (*su*), and measuring box (*masu*) to get here. The giant fir before them was the same tree often used for Christmas trees. It was an easy guess, and Masato had blurted it out in spite of himself.

And robbed Shiraaase of her life's purpose, her singular obsession, her chance to infooorm!

But Shiraaase was unperturbed. She was rather immovable to begin with, but this time her lack of emotion was downright terrifying.

"Stealing my source of joy, you naughty child. You're a very naughty child, naughty indeed. We all agree he's naughty?"

"S-sorry! I was naughty. Forgive me…"

"You admit you're naughty, then? Heh-heh-heh."

Shiraaase let out a sinister cackle and then turned to face the others once more.

"The event you're about to join is, as the naughty child said, a Christmas event. I hardly need to explain the concept of Christmas, do I?"

"A party, presents—that sorta thing, yeah?" said Wise.

"You're going to have specific groups spend time together as a family, making wonderful memories?" offered Medhi.

"Full marks for that answer! This event was proposed by a certain someone who asked to remain anonymous. We shall keep their identity a secret. Isn't that right, Mamako?"

"Yes, let's keep it secret. Hee-hee-hee."

"That explains it…hoo boy."

Unsurprisingly, Mamako was behind this. Masato glanced at her smile, shook his head, and elected not to pry further.

Then Mone raised a hand.

"Hold on! I just had a thought. It's not December twenty-fifth!"

"Right you are. But don't worry, this fir tree has a special function. If you decorate it in a manner appropriate for Christmas, the day you finish will be Christmas Eve, and the next day Christmas. It literally alters the world."

"Whoa, that's intense."

"It also has one other extremely fascinating function…three Four Kings."

"Wh-what?"

They'd been listening carefully, feigning a lack of interest, and snapped to attention when she turned toward them.

"I'll ask you first, Amante. Have you been naughty?"

"Well…yes, I have. When I think of everything I've done, I'm certainly more naughty than nice."

"How about you, Sorella? Are you a naughty child?"

"I dunno about chiiiild, but laughing at bad mothers is my goal in liiiiife, which is pretty naaaaaughty."

"Fratello, are you a naughty child?"

"Mm. No denyin' it. But I ain't no 'child'—I'm a grown man."

"So you're a naughty boy. Very well—everyone, look here."

Shiraaase knocked against the fir's trunk once more.

When she did, the giant fir began to glow. The snow-covered branches lit up from within.

The light pierced the bodies of everyone present.

Mamako was unaffected. Wise was unaffected. Medhi was unaffected.

Porta, Mone, Hahako, Shiraaase, and Dark-Mom Deathmother were unaffected.

But…

"""""…Huh?"""""

With the exception of Dark-Mom Deathmother and Shiraaase, the remaining six unaffected members all stared in surprise.

Masato, Amante, Sorella, and Fratello's gear fell to the snow. They'd vanished…

And lying in the heap of their clothing were some very surprised-looking babies, clearly less than a year old.

A Christmas Memory

Masato

Christmas, huh? You have any good Christmas stories, Wise?

Sure do. Get this! I've made my own Christmas cake. Ha-ha!

Wise

Porta

Wow! That's remarkable!

You made the cake for a Christmas party? How lovely!

Mamako

Wise

Huh? Um, no... My friends had other plans, and my dad doesn't like sweets, and my mom was out on the town so...I ate it alone...*sniff*...

Wise, use my handkerchief.

Medhi

MERRY CHRISTMAS, WISE

Chapter 2 Dah (Translation: Weren't the Libere Kings Enough? Why Me, Too?)

At the base of a giant fir tree. Masato and the Libere Kings had vanished, leaving behind piles of gear—and four stunned babies. Familiar-looking babies.

Mamako was the first to react.

"Oh dear! We can't let them lie on the snow; they'll catch cold! Hahako, hurry! We need to cradle them!"

"R-right! I can cradle a baby!"

Mamako made a beeline for the baby lying in a heap of Masato's clothing. Hahako used the white hands that spawned from all over her body to pluck all three babies out of the Kings' clothing, holding them carefully.

"I've got some baby clothing here. I know I have three, but we'll need one more... Oh, good, I did make an extra. Have them wear these."

"Mommy! Let me help!"

"I'm confused, but I can lend a hand. Let me dress one! Aw, these are so cute!"

Dark-Mom Deathmother pulled four sets of baby clothes out of her shoulder bag. Porta and Mone stepped in to help Mamako and Hahako dress the babies. Mone seemed primarily interested in how cute the clothes were.

Their swift actions ensured the babies' safety.

Now what?

"Shiraaase, what did you do?" asked Wise.

"If you confess willingly, the violence will be five percent less intense," Medhi said with a grin.

"So violence is assured either way, is it? What a terrifying girl."

Shiraaase put her hands up, surrendering.

"Let me put it this way. Christmas means presents. Presents mean Santa Claus. Which children get presents from Santa?"

"The nice ones, obviously."

"Naughty children don't get anything."

"Exactly. Naughty children get no presents! Serves them right—and yet we feel sorry for them. Such is the nature of Christmas! A day of mercy and forgiveness. So this fir tree provides them with an opportunity."

"To start over as a baby and become a good child? That's harsh!"

"It's not really forgiveness. More like a punishment...no, wait. For Hahako and the Kings, this is..."

"Right you are, Medhi. You are a clever one. Yes, by making the Libere Kings babies and having Hahako raise them, we create family memories."

Once, at the Matriarchal Arts Tournament, Mamako had told Hahako that it was memories that made them mother and son. And this was her chance to create those.

"Ohhh, so it lets the Kings gain actual experience in what having a mom is like."

"And that's why you had them join this event. Makes sense. But why did you turn Masato into a baby?"

"Personal vendetta."

"Figures."

"I'm kidding. I thought having a practical example to follow would help Hahako and her children. Don't you agree, Mamako?"

"I certainly do! I'm just so happy to be able to hold Ma-kun like this again! Tee-hee!"

She started glowing.

Mamako had Masato in a swaddle, tied to her front, and was smiling down at him.

Her joy was so great, A Mother's Light was at max brightness. "Mamako, we can't see!" "Oh, sorry." She gritted her teeth, reducing the brightness level from Sun God to Spotlight.

Hahako took her sling and put baby Amante by her belly and babies Sorella and Fratello on her back. She did this gingerly, using the white hands to make sure she didn't drop anyone.

"Aren't they heavy? I could hold one for you."

"Thank you, Mone. But I'm fine. The weight is no issue. This is the weight of happiness. Tee-hee."

"It is? Wow…"

Dark-Mom Deathmother was putting on a sling herself—

"I don't need one— I'm too big!" said Porta.

"R-right…"

—but her plan was swiftly thwarted.

The party regrouped.

"Will they ever return to normal? That is a concern, but since the main theme of this event is to create fond memories for Hahako's family, I will not address it."

"Wow, I kinda think that's the main thing on *their* minds…" said Wise.

"They're not old enough to complain. Onward with the event, then. First, we have to decorate this fir tree. We'll need ornaments, tinsel, and a star—so go forth, gather, and return here."

"Could you give us any hints on where we might find those?" asked Medhi.

"Naturally. This game is by mothers and for mothers. Making them run around while carrying babies would be just plain cruel. Fir tree, they have small children with them."

Shiraaase knocked on the trunk a third time.

The fir glowed gently. Three transport circles appeared at the base of the trunk.

"Wow! This looks fun. I think I'll tag along!" cried Mone. "Which one should I choose?"

"Whichever you please. Off you go!"

"You're not coming, Shiraaase? Slacking off on the job? Well…it is *you*," said Wise.

"Mone, you clearly misunderstand me. I'm not slacking—I have other work to do. Frankly, much of this event was implemented under some serious crunch."

"And to ensure everything goes smoothly, we've got a lot of checks to run. I'll be staying behind, too. And that means..."

Dark-Mom Deathmother turned to Porta. "Daughter!" "Mommy!" They embraced. They would have to part but would soon meet again. Soon!

This item collection quest would be handled by Mamako, Hahako, Wise, Medhi, Porta, Mone—and four babies.

"Well, everyone, let's do our best! Come on, Ma-kun! Hip, hip, hooray!"

"Dah!"

Mamako raised the baby's little hand high in the air, and they were off!

But before they could actually go anywhere, they had to check their gear and recovery items and make sure they were battle-ready.

As Mamako and the others talked things over, a fierce battle was underway near her belly.

Gah! What the hell! This is insaaaaane!

Baby Masato was extremely displeased and doing his level best to struggle—but was unable to move his arms and legs as he pleased. He was left pinned, immobile, with his face between his mother's breasts.

It was warm, soft, and smelled good. He could hear the comfortable beating of her heart, and before he knew it...

I can't sleep nowwwww! Wake uuuuup!

He tried to slap his own cheek and wake himself up. He couldn't!

This was hopeless. The only option left to baby Masato was to cry as loud as he could.

Hey! Masato Oosuki! My ears hurt! Shut up!

Wow, you're pretty loud, too! Keep it down...wait...

Amante's voice was echoing in baby Masato's head.

His vision was blurry, but he was pretty sure that was Hahako in front of him. She had baby Amante in a sling in front of her, and baby Sorella and baby Fratello on her back. All of them were staring at Masato.

What is this, some sort of telepathy? How?

Don't ask me! But at least we can communicate.

Riiiiight. So we have a favor to aaaaask...

Sonny, do something.

Look, I'd love to! But what can I do?!

Then...

"Oh my. Ma-kun's getting a little fussy! There, there."

"It's important to comfort babies when they're like this. Let me join you! There, there."

Mamako detected the problem at once and started rocking his body. Hahako joined her, rocking her body.

This was the mom skill **A Mother's Cradle**. A core technique that made you sleepier than anything else in the world.

Crap! She's gonna knock us out! Hang in there, you three! You're all about fighting mothers, so don't give in...!

Zzzzz...

They're already under! Argh...I can't hold out...zzz...

Resistance was futile.

Mamako and the others stepped into the transport circles quietly, so as not to wake the sleeping babies. Light poured out, and they were somewhere else.

The first place they went sparkled even in daylight—a town filled with signs lit up by magic stones in all seven colors. At the entrance was an especially large sign reading CASINO. The paving stones even spelled out the word. There were casinos everywhere you looked.

This was Yomamaburg, the city of Merchants, the Mecca of gamblers.

Standing at the town's entrance, Mone looked this way and that, already excited. She was jumping up and down.

"Wow! This place is crazy! So many lights!"

"I figured we'd wind up in a dungeon, but nope—a town. And *this* one."

"This place certainly opens some old wounds…"

"I had fun wearing that cute bunny girl outfit!"

Wise and Medhi would prefer to forget it. They'd poured all their money into a casino, lost a rigged match, been burdened with a crippling debt, and were forced to work for free in bunny girl outfits while serving as casino prizes.

Sorella had orchestrated their suffering, but Mamako had saved the day. The casino town was back to its usual hustle and bustle.

Now the shops all recommended gambling in pairs, parent and child, keeping an eye on each other and making sure nobody got too carried away. This had been Mamako's idea. There were lots of grown children walking the streets with their parents.

"I'm glad to see everyone is enjoying themselves safely!" said Mamako.

"I thought gambling with your mom was dumb and would only lead to violence, but I guess I was wrong. And since we're here anyway…heh-heh-heh…"

This was her chance to settle the score, and rake in some money!

Wise checked her wallet. It was empty. Sorella had already wiped her out back at the Mom Shop. She was "holding on to the money" for Wise.

"Arghhh…" Wise groaned, crestfallen.

"Wise, this is no time for playing games. We're here to find items we can use to decorate the tree."

"I—I know that, Medhi! And these aren't games…"

"Then let's get these items! But what should we go for? Where should we look?" asked Mone.

"Could they be casino prizes?" wondered Porta.

"It's possible. In that case, let's check each casino and see what prizes they're offering."

"Yes—why don't we start with that casino? It's been so long, I'd love to say hello to—oh?"

Mamako was looking down the road.

At the end of the main street was the biggest casino in all of Yomamaburg. The brightly lit, multicolored façade had a hologram of coins falling—very eye-catching.

This was where they'd met their fates. As Mamako spoke, an old man in a flawlessly tailored suit emerged. Not a face any of them would ever forget.

"Oh my! Speak of the devil. It's the manager!"

"I imagined you would be arriving soon and came out to meet you. Mamako, everyone, how lovely to see you again. I'm glad to see you're all looking well."

"You're looking well yourself, Manager. Oh, you haven't met everyone! Let me make some introductions…"

"No, that won't be necessary. If the two of you would just show me your hands…"

The manager took Hahako and Mone's hands.

There was a ding. "Oh, the Casino God." "Wow, there's a lot going on here…got it!" They both nodded.

"What did you do, Manager?"

"Mone, like myself, is an NPC. And Hahako something comparable. I simply shared the necessary data with them. A transfer paints a thousand words, as they say."

"Huh…handy. So you haven't changed much," said Wise.

"He never did care about preserving the immersion…otherwise he'd be the perfect gentleman," added Medhi.

"Ha-ha-ha, pardon me. Now then, I'm well aware of your business here! I suppose we can get right down to it."

He smiled and snapped his fingers.

Everyone vanished…

And found themselves on the stage at the center of an ancient stone arena.

"…Oh?"

"Wh-what's going on...?"

"It's a special service we offer for those with very small children. We've teleported you down to our secret casino!"

"A secret casino...but this is a combat arena, isn't it? Eep!"

Mone looked around her and saw some dirty stone chips floating by, wavering like ghosts.

This was the ancient gambling grounds. Where money, goods, and lives had been wagered and lost. The destructive impulses of the ancients remained behind, wandering aimlessly...

"The high concept is the nexus of treasure and grudges! The ghosts are merely for flair! Not frightening! Not at all! I'm totally not scared!"

Mone was shaking like a leaf.

"Whoa, calm down, Mone!"

"Hey, don't use Porta as a shield! And don't use words like *high concept* and *flair*! ...So, Manager? Why'd you bring us here?" asked Wise.

"To gamble, of course!"

The manager snapped his fingers. Beads of light appeared around the stage, expanding and transforming into a number of different objects.

Treasure chests studded with jewels, gems gleaming with magical light, silver bells—countless objects often represented as Christmas tree decorations, but real and full-sized.

"Allow me to explain the rules. These are the items you're looking for—ornaments for the giant fir tree. However, each object has a grudge attached to it and can transform into a monster—so you'll have to begin by defeating that."

"But if we attack, won't they break?"

"No worries there. These are all classified as important items, so from the game's perspective, no matter what you do to them, they'll never break."

"So we just beat up the ornament monsters? That's it?" asked Medhi.

"Of course not. You'll defeat ornaments, gather them, and then gamble with them—and take them with you only if you win that bet. Who'll be participating?"

The manager stepped to the edge of the stage, waiting for them to prepare.

"Obviously me and Medhi—Mamako, and Hahako, what do you think? I don't see how you can fight with those babies."

"But we're decorating a fir that's giant, so we need a lot of ornaments. Which would be a good time to call in their two-hit multi-target attacks…"

"That's true. This is all to make the best possible Christmas tree! Don't worry. I'll join in. And I'll keep Ma-kun perfectly safe."

"Don't worry about me, either. It would be one thing if they were ordinary babies, but they're the Heavenly Kings. Even at a time like this…see?"

The three baby Kings and baby Masato were all sleeping soundly, despite the monsters swarming around them. It didn't seem like they would be waking up anytime soon.

"Maybe they're safest while tied to the world's strongest moms. Okay, fine."

"I'll gather the ornaments! Good luck!"

"I'll help Porta! Retreating for now!"

Mone was still using Porta as a human shield. They hopped off the stage together, hiding.

The party was ready. The manager nodded and took a small bell from his pocket.

"You have five minutes to gather ornaments. Please begin!"

Ding-a-ling! He rang the bell, and the battle began.

Wise leaped forward first.

"This is a race against time! I'm going full power from the get-go! …*Spara la magia per mirare… Luce Sparo!* And! *Luce Sparo!*"

She chain cast, bursts of light firing in all directions. Peppering the ornament monsters.

When Wise got serious, she could do some incredible damage. Even the sturdiest of treasure chests were one-shot. "Collecting!" "Time to collect!" Porta and Mone scurried around, picking up all the ornaments that fell off the stage.

"Nice! I'll just keep that up! Mwa-ha-ha!"

"Wise, focus your attacks, or—"

"Relax, Medhi. I got this. No way I'm gonna hit any—*eep*?!"

She'd gotten a bit too slapdash, and a shot was sent flying directly at the manager. By the time she noticed—it was too late.

A direct hit!

"Never fear."

The light shot burst just before it struck the manager.

"Huh…?"

"In this location, no attacks against me will do any harm. This is an unbreakable rule assigned to me in my position as the Casino God. Most embarrassing."

"I see…then I suppose we don't have to worry about accidentally attacking you. *Spara la magia per mirare… Morte!*"

Medhi cast an instant death spell. A reaper appeared, split into multiple clones, and passed through the ornament monsters, tearing their grudges away.

One of them did pass through the manager—but of course, he didn't die.

"You really do cancel out all attacks… Oh, oops!"

A gem came rolling to Medhi's feet. She reflexively swung her staff like a golf club. Fore! Look out, Manager!

The gem stopped in the air right in front of him. It fell harmlessly to the ground.

"It really does cancel all attacks."

"Yo, Medhi, that was totally intentional."

"Just making sure. No malice intended. Oh, Wise, if you don't focus on the fight, they'll hog all the glory."

"Hee-hee! Yes. I might just accidentally defeat all these monsters!"

While the teens were distracted by the manager, Mamako had drawn her blades. She swung both swords gently, so as not to rock the sleeping baby Masato.

The noise of her attacks was at least 90 percent softer than usual. Stone spikes quietly shot out of the stage, water bullets silently fired, and a horde of ornament monsters were vaporized without a sound.

"Thank goodness these monsters didn't have any death cries! Ma-kun, rest easy."

"A mother's feelings can even stifle ambient noise. Allow me."

After each wave was defeated, beads of light appeared, forming more ornament monsters. It was now Hahako's turn.

She raised Terra di Madre and Altura, swinging the two Holy Swords gently…

"Wahh, wahh…"

"O-oh! My, my! Sorella woke up?!"

One of the babies on her back suddenly made a noise, and Hahako quickly turned to her.

Her swords swung with her.

The monsters weren't yet lined up properly—so all the attacks targeted the manager.

"Geez, mom attacks in this game are *so* broken!"

"Quick, cast a defensive spell! He can't possibly cancel *this* onslaught!"

Spikes that rip through any foe, water bullets that penetrate any target, all aimed at the manager!

"Fear not."

But just before they hit him, all the attacks dissipated. Even the ultimate mom attacks were powerless before him.

Everyone stared, stunned, and the manager smiled faintly. He pulled out a pocket watch.

"…Time's up. That's all the ornaments you can collect. Now it's time to gamble for the right to take them with you. I'll be your opponent!"

Porta and Mone had gathered a mountain of ornaments, a gleaming treasure horde. More than enough to decorate the giant fir. If they sold these, they could probably buy their own country. But could they take them all home?

"Let us begin."

The manager moved over to the party…and raised his fists.

"Um…when you say you'll be our opponent, you mean…literally fight?" asked Mamako.

"Yes. Fight me!"

"No, no, wait, there's no way that's a fair contest!" shouted Wise.

"You can negate all our attacks—even motherly ones—so how are we supposed to win?" demanded Medhi.

"No complaints. To arms!"

With leg strength far beyond that of his apparent age, the manager lunged toward Hahako—who was still distracted by the baby on her shoulder.

And that baby—Sorella—was his target.

"Wha—?!"

Hahako was caught completely off guard. She reacted too late. The manager's fearsome punch...

Stopped right before Sorella's eyes.

"Here we go. Rock! Paper! Scissors!"

"Dahhhh?"

The manager threw out a fist. Baby Sorella had an open palm! Or rather, she was just waving her hand around like babies do.

But she won!

"Ha-ha-ha! My loss, then. Victory is yours! Take all the ornaments with you. There's a lot, so we've prepared a special bag to transport them in."

"Wha...argh, Manager! Don't scare us like that! We seriously thought you were gonna hit her!" yelled Wise.

"You really went too far," said Medhi. "I thought my heart was going to stop."

"I do beg your pardon. But I ask for your understanding—this is an emotional issue for me, after all."

The manager held an index finger out before baby Sorella.

"Sorella, I have not forgotten what you did. You placed us under your control and did many horrible things. Demeaning mothers, making them suffer—it was hard on all of us. Even if everything ended well, we cannot forgive your actions. Thus, as the god of gambling, I charge you with an ordeal."

"Dahhh?"

It wasn't clear if she even understood his words, much less agreed to them.

But the verdict came down regardless.

"Be a child, know thy mother, and learn what happiness is. Only when you have become a loving family will I consider your sins forgiven and bless you from the bottom of my heart. That is a promise."

"Uuuu…dahhh…"

Baby Sorella's little hand reached out and wrapped around the manager's finger. Forming the old gambler's vow, "Cut my finger, if I cheat, my wealth to beat, my life shan't linger."

"I'm starting to like this manager," said Wise.

"Yeah…he's really kept our heads spinning," agreed Mone.

"Well, that is my programming."

"Do you *have* to keep bringing that up?" complained Medhi.

"Ha-ha-ha, forgive me. Hahako, I do apologize for the fuss. Take this with you. A small gift from me."

"B-but this is… Oh!"

The manager placed a small notebook in Hahako's hands. On the cover was an illustration of a mother and a baby.

"Porta! Can you appraise this? Is it what I think it is?"

"Hnggg…this is…yes! It's a maternal and child health handbook! It lets you record a child's development and serves as proof of your bonds! And if you have one of these, you can access services that help with child-rearing!"

"Isn't that lovely, Hahako? In the real world, when the doctors tell you you're pregnant, you report that to city hall, and they give you one!"

Check your local government home page for more information.

"And if you wish to take advantage of these services, they should be able to help you at any pediatrician's office!"

"That sounds marvelous! …But wait, Mamako, what's this field for?"

"Oh, that…"

Hahako had been avidly looking through the handbook, and she was pointing to a page inside.

It said…

*   *   *

Wahhhhhhhhhhhhhhhhhhhhhhhhhhhhhhh?!
  Yikes! Wh-what's going on? Was that Sorella?!
An earsplitting scream jolted baby Masato out of his slumber. But it wasn't like he could actually move.

Or really see all that well. They were indoors, at least. Mamako, Hahako, the girls, and the babies were all here.

As were a man and a woman in white. Hahako had baby Sorella on her knees, and these two were next to her, doing…something.

  Augh! That hurts! I'm dying!
  Dying? Why? What's going on?
  Masato Oosuki, calm down. It's no big deal.
  Mm. Sorella's just bein' a big baby. Pathetic.
  You sure this is 'no big deal'…?
Even as the babies communicated telepathically, the situation was progressing rapidly.

Still wailing, baby Sorella was passed over to Medhi. Wise had been holding on to Amante, and she stepped forward, placing the baby on Hahako's knees.

It was baby Amante's turn.

  Ha! Sorella always had the weakest defense in the Libere Rebellion. This won't work on meeeeeaghhhhhhhhhhhhhhhhhhhhhhhhhhhhhhh?!
  Whoa? That sounds like it really hurts?
Baby Masato couldn't see well enough to tell what was going on.

Baby Fratello was up next. Mone stepped forward, placing her on the lap of doom.

  I'm a proud member of the Rebellion! Y'all won't catch me wailing like aughhhhhhhhhhhhhhhhhhhhhhhhhhhhhhhhhhhhhhhhhhhhhhhhhhhhhh hhhhhhhhhhhhhhhhhhhhhhhhhhhhhhhhhhhhhhhhhhhhhhh?!
  You're the loudest one yet?! Why?! What are they doing to you?
Hahako stood up, patting baby Fratello, soothing her wails.

This meant it was finally Masato's turn. "Ma-kun, you can do it!"

He was plunked down on Mamako's lap, the sleeve of his baby clothes rolled up. All ready.

The lady in the white clothes—from this distance, he could tell she was a nurse—dampened a cotton ball with disinfectant and rubbed it lightly on baby Masato's arm.

Wait...does this mean...oh, okay. That explains it.

The man in white smiled and leaned in with a hypodermic needle.

Yes. A shot.

Geez, I'm not gonna scream about a dumb shot. You girls are pathetic. Lemme show you how it's done. I'm not gonna bat an eye. I'll endure this like the hero I am!

He might be a baby, but this was a chance to show off. He was gonna be the *best* baby.

He could handle it. Shots weren't scary. A confident smirk appeared on baby Masato's lips.

Poke.

"Aiiiiiiiiiiiiiiiiiiiiiiiiiiiiiiiiiiiiiiiiiiieeeeeeeeeeeeeeeeeeeeeeeeeeeeeeeeeeeeee eeeeeeeeeeeeeeeeeeeeeeeeeeeeeeeeeeeeeeeeeeeeeeeeeeeeeeeeeeeeeeeeeeeeeeeeeee eeeeeeeeeeeeeeeeeeeeeeeeeeeeeeeeeeeeeeeeeeeeeeeeeeeeeeeeeeeeeeeeeeeeeeeeeee eeeeeeeeeeeeeeeeeeeeeeeeeeeeeeeeeeeeeeeeeeeeeeeeeeeeeee?!"

"Oh my! That hurt, didn't it? Hang in there. This will keep you from getting sick! There, there, don't cry, don't cry."

"Wow, Masato cried louder than anyone!"

"Geez, knock it off... I'm getting a headache..."

"How can such a little body make so much noise..."

"I know he's a baby and can't help it, but...ohhh..."

"Sorry, everyone. But shots are important. Forgive him."

The chorus of four crying babies was so loud, it seemed like the glass in the exam room was about to shatter.

Mamako smiled though it all. Hahako was busy describing their crying in her handbook. The other girls all covered their ears with both hands, scowling.

Vaccines come in many forms and have to be given on specific schedules. Consult your doctor and local government guidelines for more information!

They'd obtained their ornaments.

After soothing the crying babies with A Mother's Cradle, the party returned to the giant fir.

But decorating would have to wait until they had everything they needed. They put the ornament bag down. "Daughter!" "Mommy!" They allowed Porta and her mother time to hug, then they were on the move again.

The next transport circle took them to a town called Meema. This was where the Matriarchal Arts Tournament had been held.

Mamako's party landed on the stage where the mothers had fought, at the center of the main hall, surrounded by monuments to cooking and cleaning supplies.

"Oh my! I remember this!"

"Mamako, this was where I first met you, fought you, and became who am I today. This place is important to me. And yet…"

There was not a soul in the stands. A hush lay over the arena—and there was a chill in the air.

They looked up at the sky and saw it covered in dark clouds. Every now and then they could hear the rumble of thunder.

"…Thaaaat doesn't seem promising," said Wise.

"Yeah. Like it's about to rain…or a monster's about to attack."

"I think you just jinxed us all, Mone…" said Medhi.

There *was* something out there. Like a snake, but no ordinary snake—far too long and thick, covered in some sort of silvery hairs. They could just make it out between the gaps in the clouds.

"Hngg! That's a monster! The body is covered in tinsel! It's a kind of dragon known as a Tinselron!"

"Wait, a *real* monster?! A *dragon*?! That thing's the real deal!"

"Mone, what were you thinking?! We're in the middle of a town! I can't believe you."

"If we fight here, collateral damage will be unavoidable. How are you going to pay for all that?"

"Auughhhhh?! Is this really my fault? It isn't, right? Please say it isn't!"

Mone grabbed their sleeves, but Wise and Medhi turned their backs on her. "We don't know you." "This sin is yours alone." "Noooo!" Good-bye, Mone. Your cell is this way...

But before she could be incarcerated...

"Relax! It's not your fault!"

A figure leaped from the top of the gate between the stage and the waiting rooms.

She spun magnificently through the air, landing in front of them...a middle-aged woman, fully humanoid except for the dog ears and tail. A beastkin.

She, too, had been in the Matriarchal Arts Tournament.

"Oh my! Growlette!"

"It's been far too long, Mamako. Wise, Medhi, Porta...and a new face, and some faces I know but that have gotten much smaller since the last time I saw them."

"Oh, you noticed? This is Masato! It's a long story."

"It isn't often that we see you without your kids, Growlette."

"Yeah, I was forced to leave them with someone. More important..." The beastkin mother scowled over at Hahako, who shifted uncomfortably. "You look exactly like Mamako, so I assume you're Hahako. The one who made a mess of the Matriarchal Arts Tournament and tried to steal my children. I haven't forgotten."

"Neither have I...but I've no idea how to even begin apologizing."

"Wait, Growlette. Hahako is no longer—"

"Let me handle this, Mamako. I've got something she needs to hear. First..."

Growlette pushed Mamako aside and reached for Hahako...

And tightened the loose string on her sling.

"If you wanna be a proper mom, you gotta keep an eye on these things! You can't go dropping your babies!"

"Th-thank you."

"I recognize these kids, too—not in a good way, either. I'd love to hear exactly what led up to this...but it'll have to wait."

There was an earsplitting monstrous roar, and Tinselron's face appeared through the clouds.

There were six eyes surrounded by silver scales, each glittering like a dangerous gem, fixed on the prey on the stage below.

"Sorry, but can you lend a hand? If we don't do something about that monster, it'll be a real disaster!"

"Okay, you got it! Let's show Growlette how much our skills have leveled up!"

"Porta and Mone—oh, and Mamako and Hahako, step back. We can't have the babies distracting you during this fight."

Wise and Medhi stepped forward. This was the magical girls' time to shine!

But Tinselron attacked first, shaking all the hairs on its body. A most unpleasant rustling.

Wise's magic was sealed. Medhi had instantly used her as a shield, but her magic was sealed, too.

"Predictable. I figured that would happen any minute now." Wise smiled.

"Yes. As did I. It's almost a relief to get it over with." Medhi smiled.

"You've gotten way better at accepting the harshness of reality! But this ain't no time for games! I could take him out with one swing, but I can't reach him that high. If someone doesn't back me up..."

"Then this is Ma-kun's moment! Yay!"

Masato was sound asleep in the sling, but Mamako lifted his fist up for him, stepping forward.

"Wait, Mamako...don't be ridiculous! What can a baby do? Step back, it's dangerous!"

"Don't worry, Growlette. Ma-kun is the warrior chosen by the heavens. He'll unleash an amazing power! ...Porta, dear, do you have a moment?"

"Y-yes? What is it?"

With Porta's help, Mamako...

...placed a baby bed on the center of the stage, set Masato on it, and lay down next to him!

Then...!

"Night night. Night night. Night night. Night...night...*zzz*..."

Masato was already asleep, but Mamako tried to settle him down... and fell asleep herself. Everyone stared, flabbergasted.

The special mom skill A Mother's Nap activated!

This occurs when a mother accidentally falls asleep trying to put her baby to bed! Mother and child sleep side by side, looking ever so peaceful! A great calm falls over all who bear witness to the sight!

A moment later, there was a whoosh from the sky above. Tinselron had fallen asleep, and was falling toward them!

"Well, I see she's as nuts as ever. Blows your mind!"

Growlette thrust her claws into Tinselron's neck, and the dragon was slain.

When Tinselron's body vanished, a huge pile of silver tinsel was left behind.

Which meant...

"...Y'know, Masato didn't actually *do* anything," said Mone.

"Yeah...he was asleep from start to finish. That's basically the definition of 'not doing anything.'"

"But if Mamako says this was his doing, I suppose we can give him the credit."

"Yes! Masato wins!"

The baby hero scored a great victory, and they had all the tinsel they needed to decorate the giant fir.

Everyone worked together to stuff the long tinsel strands into Porta's shoulder bag, and then they left the Matriarchal Arts Tournament arena behind.

As they walked, they explained how four of them had ended up

becoming babies, and what had brought them here. They were headed toward the end of the road, where the city guard barracks were.

Once there, they paused before the entrance. Growlette straightened herself up.

"My children have caused no end of trouble for you," she said. "My deepest apologies."

She bowed low to the guards, who were looking distinctly uncomfortable in their matching armor.

The captain of the guards sighed deeply through his whiskers.

"Fortunately, there was no damage to the town—so we'll ask no further questions about Tinselron's arrival. But make sure the other guardians know to be on the lookout. We don't want situations like this occurring again."

"Yes. I promise. And sorry."

"Hold on—what's all this about Tinselron and your kids?" Wise asked.

The captain's frown deepened.

Growlette hung her head.

"Tinselron was a rare monster prepared for a Christmas event being held in secret. Summoned by the seven balls hidden in this town, you obtain a vast quantity of tinsel by defeating him. But…Growlette here just happened to be passing through…"

"And my children found all the balls hidden in this city, and then curiosity got the best of them…"

"And they summoned the dragon? Yeah, those five troublemakers would totally do that. But we're trying to get through those events, and we got the tinsel we needed, so…we're good. Right, Captain?"

"Yes—that's a satisfactory solution. As far as Tinselron is concerned." He glanced over his shoulder, looking very tired.

Behind him…

"Pway wiff us!" "Pway!" "Hugs!" "Arm swings!" "Up!"

"Hahh….hahh…I can't…I'm only human…"

"We're not as strong or as tough as beastkin! Please…have mercy…"

"Then let's draw!" "Draw!" "Art!" "Crayons!" "Look!"

"Wait, not there! You can't draw on the walls!"

"Or that paper! That's an important docu—augh, too late."

It was basically a crime scene. There were scribbles *everywhere*. One chair leg was broken, and a window was cracked...

Like it had been through the eye of a storm. Five beastkin children racing all around, ears twitching, tails wagging. And the young soldiers were slumped on the ground, utterly exhausted.

The color drained from Growlette's face. She looked ready to turn to ash.

"K-kids?! Wh-wh-what are you doing? Stop that! Come here! Line up! Say you're sorry! Now!"

"Huh?" "No." "Pway wiff us!" "Hugs!" "Mommy, hugs!"

"No hugs! Say you're sorry! Mommy's really mad!"

She struck a proper mother scolding stance.

It was like a crackle of electricity running down each kid's spine. They quickly threw themselves at her.

"We're sorry!" "Mommy, I'm sorry!" "Sorry!" "Forgive us!" "Sowwy!"

"Not to me! They're the ones you bothered! Go on!"

""""""Sorry!""""""

"They just pile it on, don't they? I can't apologize enough!"

Growlette and the beastkin kids all bowed their heads in unison.

The entire family's tails and ears were drooping. The captain let out a long sigh and then said, "Apology accepted. That's enough! Raise your heads."

"Th-thank you! Thank you! I'll pay for everything they broke! And I'll clean!"

"Nah, won't be necessary," the captain said. "The paperwork...we can redo. And this guard station is scheduled to be replaced soon. So a little dirt and damage isn't an issue."

"Replace?" "First I've heard of it..." The other guards looked puzzled. Suspicious.

His men glared at him, but he shushed them and shrugged.

"Just talking to myself here, but my son's a student, you see. And he got mixed up in this attempted coup at the adventurer academy he attends. But the teachers forgave children and parents alike, not a word of rebuke."

He turned to Mamako, the one who'd resolved the situation, and saluted.

Then he grinned.

"Kids were born to cause trouble. And as a parent myself, I've gotta be as forgi*ving* as my own son was forgi*ven*. Everyone cool with that?"

"No complaints here!" "Bad ass, Captain!" "Your wife's got you under her thumb!"

"Ha-ha-ha, who said that?!"

He grabbed the culprit and pulled him into a cobra twist. "Choke! Choke!" "Who cares?!" What a violent way to hide embarrassment.

Growlette bowed her head several more times, and when she looked up, she wiped the tears from her eyes.

"Then at least let me clean! Will that be okay?"

"Fine. Knock yourself out."

"Then we'll help! The more hands, the faster the work goes!"

"Okay...Porta, you're up!"

"Yes! Leave this to me!"

Everyone grabbed rags, brooms, dusters, all the cleaning supplies they needed to make the guard station spick-and-span. Paperwork was organized, and scribbles washed away.

Wise and Medhi went into big sister mode, teaching the beastkids how to clean. Nearby, "Porta, can you help with this?" "Yes!" Porta was secretly using Item Creation to replace the broken chair and window.

As they worked, Growlette quietly placed herself next to Hahako.

"Guess it's pretty clear I ain't exactly a perfect mom myself. We make trouble, apologize, and beg forgiveness. I ain't got no right to hold a grudge against you."

"...You'll forgive my failures at the Matriarchal Arts Tournament?"

"That's what I'm saying, yeah. And for everything those Rebellion kids you've got sleeping on your back did. Back in the beastkin world, Materland, they sank a whole dang island! Fortunately, nobody died.

Honestly, no one's really mad. We wound up with a great place to play!"

Exploring the sunken Libere Rebellion base had become a really popular skin-diving tour—but that's a topic for another day.

With three babies to look after, Hahako wasn't at her most mobile, so Growlette straightened up the paperwork for her and then turned to look her in the eye.

"You gonna make those girls your daughters?"

"Yes. That is my wish."

"Then remember this. Kids make mischief. No matter what. The important part is how you handle it. You've gotta be there for them."

"I know…and let me apologize. For what I did, and for what they've done. I'm very sorry."

Hahako bowed her head carefully, to the extent that the babies allowed it.

As she moved to write this advice down in her handbook…

"Mah…" Baby Fratello's bleary eyes fluttered open.

It was probably just a noise to her, but it felt like a baby's first word.

"Oh, are you sorry, too?" asked Growlette. "Well said, kiddo. You all have to be good girls and help your mother out."

"Mah."

"Good answer!"

Growlette took it as one anyway. So everyone else did, too.

She patted baby Fratello softly on the cheek.

At any rate, they'd obtained the second decorative item—silver tinsel.

When they'd finished cleaning, the party said good-bye to Growlette and returned to the giant fir tree. They placed the tinsel to one side—"Daughter!" "Mommy!" And waited out a second round of Porta family hugs.

Mone was watching them, biting a finger.

"Lucky! I want some kids. I need to stock up on spoiling! But Masato's a baby, and Mamako's busy with Masato…"

"Fine, I'll spoil you. C'mere!"

"It's necessary to restrain your powers, right? Come, then."

Wise and Medhi both gave their saintliest smiles and spread their arms wide.

"I'm good, thanks."

""Hey!""

Apparently they didn't meet the baseline spoiler qualifications.

There was now a snow hut by the side of the giant fir and a kotatsu inside. On the kotatsu was a work tablet, a portable grill, a portable burner, and a pot.

On the grill's grates was some mochi, puffing up nicely.

"That looks good! I was just feeling peckish."

"For all your talk about work, you sure know how to treat yourself, Shiraaase."

"I *am* working. But it is almost noon."

"We've prepared these both as lunch and as a means of acquiring the sugar that keeps our brains functioning. There's enough for all of you. Take a break from item gathering and join us."

"Yes! I would love some! I love eating the lunch Mommy made!"

"I-I-I'm glad to hear it! Here's an extra piece of mochi for my adorable daughter!"

Dark-Mom Deathmother's glasses had fogged up from the vapors of love for her daughter, but at this point everyone was just leaving them to it.

They had *shiruko* for lunch. Topped with beautifully grilled mochi. Everyone dug in.

"""""Mmmm!""""" Squeals of joy echoed through the snow hut.

Then…

……*Mm? That smells good!*

In Mamako's arms, baby Masato's eyes opened.

He couldn't see that well, but he could still make out the *shiruko*. They were eating *shiruko*! In a snow hut!

This was definitely the sort of dish that tasted ten times better in the right environment. Everyone was clearly enjoying it accordingly.

"Enh…gwehhhhhhh! (Hey, where's my *shiruko*? Let me have some!)"

"Yikes! Masato suddenly started crying! Crap, he's loud!"

"Waaaaaaaaaaaaaaaaaaaaah! (Sorry! I'm not trying to be this loud!)"

Baby Masato was just trying to talk normally, but that didn't appear to be an option. No matter what he said, it came out as a bawl.

"That's quite the voice… I wonder if Masato's hungry?"

"Yaahhhhhhhhhhhh! (Right you are, Mone! Yes, that's my point here!)"

"Or maybe he just needs his diaper changed!"

"Gahhhhhhh! (Damn it, Medhi, no! That's not it!)"

"I don't smell anything. I think he's doing just fine…"

"Eeeeeeaughhh! (Great, Mom! You know best! Feed me!)"

"Well, if it seems fine, all the more reason to make a visual check. Not like in a weird way. I don't mean it like that."

"Eeeeeeeek?! (Yo, Wise?! Have you lost it?! Are you literally insane?!)"

But despite Masato's screams, Wise plucked him out of Mamako's arms and laid him down on the kotatsu.

"Come, Mamako!" "Yes, just a quick check." "Aiiiieeee?! (No, stop?!)" It was just a check. Absolutely nothing weird about it.

Mamako peeled back the baby clothes and then opened baby Masato's diaper all the way.

ω

"It does look like a garlic clove." *Staaaare.*

"There's definitely a resemblance." *Staaaaare.*

"Garlic glove, indeed." *Staaaare.*

"I-I'm not looking!" *Glance.*

"Hm, approximately two centimeters." *Staaaare.*

He was just a baby. Nothing to be embarrassed about.

Shiraaase had quietly joined the row of girls, armed with a ruler, making all the proper measurements. There were no problems with the diaper. It was placed back in full lockdown.

Baby Masato did seem a bit dead-eyed, like his soul had left his body, but Mamako picked him up again.

"Then he must be hungry! Does anyone mind if I feed him here?"

"Go ahead. It's just girls here, and none of us are going to complain."

"Thank you, Deathmother. Here we go, Ma-kun!"

"Wah? Wahhhhhhhhhhhhhhhhhhh?! (Wh-what are you talking aboooooout?!)"

Mamako had undone the front of her dress and popped out her right boob.

There was nothing strange about this. It was how mothers fed babies! *No wait, wait, wait, wait! It's not* wrong, *but just…don't!*

Mamako's boob was coming in hot! It was bigger than baby Masato's head!

"I'm probably wrong here, but do you think Masato's mind is still in there? Like, his normal teenage mind?" asked Wise.

"If that was true, this would be a real mess," said Medhi. "Perhaps it's different in other cultures, but in Japan, a high school boy breast-feeding is…well, it would certainly go down in history for Heroic Sons. They'd sing songs about it for eons to come."

"I dunno, maybe we should report this or something?" offered Mone.

"Er…I'm not sure myself!" said Porta.

The girls were all watching avidly. And the fateful moment arrived! Baby Masato's little mouth closed around Mamako's—!

"The teat of fate! I do hate to interrupt this momentous occasion, but Mamako, do you actually have any milk in there?" asked Shiraaase.

"Oh my! Good point. I definitely don't."

Standard breast milk is produced after a birth. Baby Masato had not been born recently, merely babified by the magic of the giant fir tree.

Just to be sure, Mamako gave her boob a solid squeeze, but failed to lactate.

"I figured this might happen, so I prepared some milk. We made it before the *shiruko*…it should be warm enough by now. Here."

"Thank you, Ms. Shiraaase. It's such a help."

"Wahhhh! (Seriously, you're a life saver.)"

Having overcome the greatest crisis of his Heroic Son career, Masato was given a bottle.

And thus he was safely fed. "You owe me one," Shiraaase whispered, but he pretended not to hear. This was all her fault in the first place.

While this was going on, the baby Kings awoke. "Hahako!" "Emergency!" "Yes, leave it to me." Three sobbing babies were given bottles, which they drained quickly. Chug-chug.

"Well, Ma-kun. Once you've eaten…"

"*Urp.* (Whoops, 'scuse me.)"

To avoid building up gas, he was held up against her shoulder and given several back pats. The burp signaled the end of mealtime.

"Ma-kun, you ate all your food! You're such a good boy!"

"All three of you finished your meals. Good girls, each one of you."

Once they were fed, the babies quickly drifted off to sleep. Baby Masato on Mamako's chest, the three Kings in Hahako's arms, every eye drifting shut.

Meanwhile, the rest of the party polished off the *shiruko* and gave thanks—for all kinds of things.

Then…

"My? This is unexpected!"

"Oh dear! What is this?"

Baby Masato's body had suddenly pulsed and was getting bigger. So were the baby Kings. Arms and legs stretching, baby clothes buttons bursting, ripping…

They'd gone from less than a year old to toddler-sized!

"…Mm? Wait…am I bigger?"

"You are! You look…three years old! I'm sure of it."

"Eating right and having your mother call you a good child seems to have helped you all grow up! You might even be three centimeters now."

"Augh! *What* might be three centimeters?! You're weird, Shiwaaashe!"

Time to get them dressed.

*　　*　　*

As long as Dark-Mom Deathmother was around, they didn't lack for materials. She soon had clothes for all the kids.

Three-year-old Amante got a skirt and a child-sized stadium jacket with a tiger-striped kitty embroidered on the back.

Three-year-old Sorella got a short dress and a hat with a cute skull mark.

Three-year-old Fratello got shorts and a hoodie with a goofy-looking shark on it.

"I picked these clothes for you... Do you like them?"

"Humph. Good enuff."

"I thiiiink...I might liiiike them."

"Ain't too shabby."

The outfits all paid homage to their full-sized quirks, which seemed to please them.

Hahako seemed relieved. She had a measuring tape and was sneakily writing their heights in her notebook. Recording her children's growth.

Meanwhile, three-year-old Masato. Shorts and a jacket—typical activewear for a young boy.

But the illustration on the back of the jacket was a Baumkuchen cake.

"You're the hero of the heavens, Ma-kun, so I made it a Baumkuchen! Do you like the clothes Mommy picked out?"

"Nngh, I dun get it...b-but I'm a good boy, so I'm not gonna compwain... Argh! I wanna grow up!"

They were too little to equip weapons. The children were all ready to head out.

"Then let's go get the final decoration item," said Shiraaase. "Good luck, three centi—I mean, Masato."

"Augh! Let'sh get dis event over with sho I can grow up."

"Oh my, Ma-kun! You can't go off alone. Make sure you hold Mommy's hand."

"I dun need to! I'm fine on my own!"

The Oosukis, the teenage girls, the toddler Kings, and Hahako all set out merrily, stepping into the transport circle. They were enveloped in light.

As they faded from sight, Shiraaase and Dark-Mom Deathmother sighed.

"Only one thing left. It's all going well."

"Yes. Almost there. Not much longer until the beautiful ending, when Hahako and those girls become a real family."

"...Mind if point out something unnecessarily?"

"I'd prefer you didn't."

"You didn't say a word to those girls at all while they ate. Are you sure you're okay with that?"

"I said, don't point it out! Argh. All they need is a mother who raised them. There's no place for their failure of a birth mother here."

"You got all branches of management mixed up in this, begging for our help, worked yourself till you were covered in tears, but okay. I just thought they ought to know how much of yourself you poured into this event."

Shiraaase looked her way, but Dark-Mom Deathmother avoided her eyes.

"No point addressing it. Let's get these system checks done. Can't have anything going wrong. We must be cautious—hm?"

She'd just noticed Mone, standing alone in the transport circle.

Her hands clasped before her belly. She looked lost in thought.

"Mone? Is something wrong?"

"Er? Oh, uh...I ate with everyone, but I don't feel full...ah, it's nothing. Just a little hungry!"

"Then have some more mochi. We've got plenty."

Deathmother took some mochi from the grill and sandwiched it between some seaweed—a dish known as isobeyaki.

Mone took a bite and flashed a bright smile. When she stepped back on the circle, she was transported, too.

"A healthy appetite. The wonders of youth."

"Yes…let's hope that's all it is."

Dark-Mom Deathmother went back to the snow hut, focused on her tablet.

Meanwhile, Shiraaase stayed where she was, staring at the circle Mone had used.

The third transport put them on a hill overlooking the sea.

A crescent-moon-shaped coastline, a port town with orange roofs, ships with white sails. All these things drew the eye, but nothing so much as the tower looming over them on an island in the bay.

This was the coastal city, Thermo. A village known for its tower dungeon.

"Sorry I'm late!" *Munch, munch.*

"What kept you, Mone? …Oh, never mind. Guess it's obvious."

"Everyone's here! Let's get going."

"Yes! Let's get da last item!"

Masato was all fired up. This was how he was going to finish growing. He ran off on his three-year-old legs…

And immediately tripped and fell.

"Wah! Masato, are you okay?" asked Porta.

"Unh…i-it doeshn't hurt…it's jusht sho *shad*. I wanna cry."

Sniff.

"C'mon, Masato. Don't be so stubborn! Just hold Mamako's hand," said Wise.

"If we have to stop every time you fall down, we'll never get anywhere. You'll end up being stuck as a child for much longer," said Medhi.

"Mommy doesn't mind that at all! Tee-hee!"

"I mind! …F-fine! Jusht for now! Got dat?"

"Yes. Take Mommy's hand, okay?"

He held out his little hand, and hers wrapped around it. Soft, smooth, and warm. Just holding hands made him feel safe and protected.

Meanwhile, Hahako and her kids…

"Holding handsh meansh no twipping. So let's do dat. Sowella, Fwa-tello, come on!"

Toddler Amante in the middle, three-year-old Sorella on the right, and three-year-old Fratello on the left. The trio walked off, hand in hand.

"If we can walk on our own, we won't need Mommy'sh help! Dun want it! Humph!"

"Uhhh, maaaaaaybe."

"Mm. Maybe."

"Oh dear. How sad. When you were babies, I carried you all the time. But now that you're a little bigger, you want more space. *Sniff.*"

Hahako followed after them, looking so, so sad. Ready to cry.

Or so it seemed.

Toddler Sorella and toddler Fratello were actually using their free hands to hold on to Hahako—but making sure three-year-old Amante couldn't see. They were latched on to her wrist and the hem of her skirt, so it was a one-sided hold, but the link was there. Hahako was grinning.

The transformation wasn't complete, but it was definitely there, to a surprising degree.

"...Mommy, what's goin' on with dem?"

"A lot happened while you were asleep, Ma-kun."

"Hmm..."

Toddler Masato wanted to know more but felt like prying might ruin it. He decided to keep quiet and watch.

The party set out down the hill, into the sea-breeze-scented streets of Thermo.

Looking for information, they first headed for the Adventurers Guild Mamako had founded to clear the tower dungeon, the Mom Guild. But on the way...

"Right, on my signal, give it a pull! One, two!"

""""Heave, ho! Heave, ho!""""

There was a familiar rough-hewn man's voice, followed by children's voices shouting together.

There was a crowd by the cliff. Mostly women and young children. Lots of families.

A chubby woman with a perm noticed them approaching and waved from the middle of the crowd.

"Oh, if it isn't Mamako! Yoo-hoo!"

"Oh…my, my, if isn't Pocchi's mother! And so many other Mom Guild members here, too!"

They'd all conquered the tower dungeon together. And just the other day, when young adventurers had attacked, seeking the elimination of all mothers, they'd held the line and fended them off. These battle-hardened powerhouse moms all came running toward Mamako.

And suddenly…

"Mamako, it's been ages! Oh my, is that Masato?"

"It is! It's a long story. Ma-kun, say hi!"

"I'm Masato Oosuki. I'm thwee years old! …No, wait, there'sh no time to chat—"

"Wise, Medhi, Porta! How nice to see you all again. Have you been well?"

"Y-Yeah…" "Thankfully…" "I'm great!"

"We've got tea and treats! Will you join us? Oh, are these your friends?"

"Why, you look just like Mamako! Oh, so you must be the famous—"

"Hahako. A pleasure to meet you."

"And are those your children? Oh, they're so cute!"

"Hey, what'sh da big idea?" "Too many moooothers!" "Sho loud…!"

"Can you introduce yourselves? Names and ages?"

They didn't even leave enough room for the wind to pass between the chatter. They were doomed. Worst-case scenario, they'd be stuck here for over an hour, helpless to free themselves.

But an opportunity presented itself. The mothers had been interested in toddler Masato, but their eyes soon drifted upward, and the discussion focused on Mamako.

And then Mamako let go of Masato to accept a proffered cookie.

…Yes! Now!

Three-year-old Masato carefully slipped between the mothers' legs, wriggling free of the net. He'd successfully escaped—

Or so he thought. Someone grabbed his arm, pulling him back!

"Masato Oosuki, jusht you wait! No eshcaping!"

"Oh, you guys are here, too? Fine! Come on!"

"Quietlyyyy! Sho we dun get cauuuught!"

"Let'sh run for it!"

The three-year-old Kings had also escaped—they formed a new team. Together, they sneaked away.

Watchful of the mothers' eyes, they headed right for the beach. There, they found a huge crowd of children. As adults yelled instructions, the children pulled on a long rope that stretched into the ocean waves.

"Masato Oosuki! What are those people doin'?"

"Net fishing, maybe? You throw a net in da water and pull it out, and there's fish and shellsh inshide."

"Fishiiiing? Ohhh…that sounds fuuun!"

"Mm. Good back mushcle workout."

"You all want to join in, then? This is an event for parents and children, sponsored by the Mom Guild. All kids have a right to participate!"

There came a gruff voice behind them, and rough-hewn hands patted their heads.

They turned around and found a very suspicious man crouching behind them. Bulging muscles, a mohawk, and a face only a mother could love.

"Oh? Pocchi?"

"Yo, Masato. It's been a minute since we last met—you got real tiny."

This was the leader of a gang of former thugs who were now part of the Mom Guild. The son of Pocchi's mother—which meant his name, logically, was Pocchi.

"I heard the mothers kicking up a fuss, so I knew you were here, but I didn't count on you looking like this! Still…"

Pocchi gave Amante a long, hard look.

"Yo, Amante. You worked us to the bone, turned us into monsters, and then cast us aside. You were a leader in the evil Rebellion...and now? Look at you! You're so cute!"

"Tch...wh-what? You tink you can beat me now? Out for revenge? Fine! Let'sh fight!"

"Revenge? Yeah, I suppose you got some payback coming your way, but...don't be ridiculous. I ain't raising a hand to a little kid! That goes against my policy...as a childcare worker."

Pocchi stood up, puffing up his chest proudly.

His apron had a cute gorilla on it. It flapped in the wind.

"Er...P-Pocchi? You're a childcare worker?"

"The Mom Guild started a day care! I'm currently doing training to get my license. There are way too many fools out there who don't know how lucky they are to have moms. I figured the best way to teach them the truth was to start when they're small. Got that, Amante?"

"Wh-what?"

"First, you gotta let yourself be held with love."

"Huh?"

"Just like how I woke from a bad dream when my mother put her arms around me. A good hug can work miracles! It's high time you accepted that mothers ain't going anywhere and become a good girl!"

His muscles rippled.

"Eeeeeeeeeeeeek?!"

Pocchi's burly bro smile of love advanced on three-year-old Amante! "Call da poliiiiice!" "Mm." "I'll help!" It reeked of criminal activity, but it was mere wholesome education! Pure early childhood learning! All charges would likely be dropped...

But then...

"Yo, Pocchi! Over here! Emergency!"

"Huh? What? What's going on?"

Another thuggish-looking man—like Pocchi, wearing a day-care worker's apron—came running toward them, looking distraught.

"The net got stuck, so I dove in to take a look! But there's a monster I've never seen before caught in it! It's really huge!"

"What?! We can't just stand here! Get these kids—"

But before he could even finish...

The surface of the ocean exploded, a column of water rocketing upward like a geyser. A gold, glittering, star-shaped monster emerged from the blue waters of the ocean.

A giant starfish, the size of a ship's sail. It was moving its five arms like wings, fluttering over the water's surface.

"Ooh! A fwying monster! That's mine!"

"Masato, don't be stupid. You're too small to fight this thing! Everyone, run! C'mon, Amante! You too."

"Eeeeeeeek?!"

Pocchi scooped up toddler Masato and toddler Amante, and the distraught childcare worker scooped up toddler Sorella and toddler Fratello. With a three-year-old under each arm, they ran off. "Over here!" "Hurry!" Porta and Mone were beckoning furiously. The children pulling the net were snatched up by their guardians, and everyone hastily fled the beach.

They were replaced by Mamako's party, who ran out toward the surf, ready for combat.

"Oh dear! It's so big and sparkly!"

"A gold star—and exactly the right size to decorate that giant fir. Is this another decoration item?"

Both mothers had quietly made certain their precious children had been safely evacuated, and they were now ready to lead the assault. Two Holy Swords of the Ocean swung together.

A double layer of water bullets hit home, and the giant starfish split into five. Now they had five starfish, each the size of a dinghy.

"Yikes, there's more of 'em! I hate this type of monster..."

"Well, we'll just have to burn off the excess calories we consumed!"

"From the looks of it, the smaller ones are easier to handle! Which means... *Spara la magia per mirare... Luce di Lampo!*"

Wise's spell activated! A sphere of lightning appeared, then burst, and the scattered bolts struck all the starfish.

Once again, they divided. Each split into five more starfish, each of those the size of a human child. Twenty-five in all.

The child-sized starfish began spinning like shuriken, arms sharp as blades. They attacked, but— "Not happening!" Medhi instantly deployed a defensive wall, fending them off.

A lot of enemies. It would take a lot of hands to defeat them—as many hands as the starfish had arms.

"We'll fight, too! Mom Guild company—charge!"

"""Aye-aye!"""

My kids, your kids, all kids are good kids. The maternal need to protect all kids gave them strength, and that strength became armor, covering their bodies—the armor of moms, Full Armom.

Now combat ready, the army of moms grabbed on to the child-sized starfish, embracing them. "Tee-hee, boys, boys, be good." "Aiiiiieeee?!" The starfish all screamed but then went limp. Much like Pocchi had back in the day.

Meanwhile, all the toddlers could do was stand around watching.

"Finally, a fight! And I can't do nothin'! Argh!"

"Not much you can do at this age! Behave yourself."

"Hey! Let go of me, Pecchi! Leggo before I get really mad!"

"You settle down now. And it's Pocchi, not Pecchi."

Pocchi had settled down cross-legged a safe distance from the coast, his bulging biceps acting as seat belts to restrain toddlers Masato and Amante.

Meanwhile, the other thug childcare worker was taking care of three-year-old Sorella and Fratello. His ugly mug seemed to terrify them both, so they were being quiet as mice.

Amante was trying to escape, but Pocchi made her sit, keeping a close eye on the combat in front of them.

"Masato, that lady who looks just like Mamako—that's Hahako, right? I've heard the rumors."

"Uh, yeah. She ish. She'sh a…shpecial pershon. She'sh tryin' real hard to become a mommy to Amante and da other Libere Kingsh."

"Argh, Masato Oosuki! Don't tell *him* dat!"

"Ohh? That is a special lady. Who'd wanna be a mom to these kids? Guess it takes all types."

"Pocchi, dat's jusht mean…"

"Truth hurts. I mean, they're the last people in the world that would ever love a mother. No saving them, right? They're unsalvageable."

Pocchi gave three-year-old Amante a grin that was clearly trying to wind her up. She scowled back up at him.

"Did I say anything wrong? You don't even know *how* to be a good girl. Right?"

"You think I'm dat eashy? Shure, I'm pisshed off. But nothing. Will ever. Make me shay what you want. I won't shay 'I'll prove I can be a good girl.'"

"Tch, you might look like a kid, but you don't think like one, huh?"

His bait had failed. But Pocchi wasn't giving up that easy.

"Well, if you ain't a kid anymore, you oughta be able to do better. Grow out of this sort of thing."

"Too bad! I'm opposed to all mothersh. Dat's what I wash deshigned to be. It'sh how I wash made. I can't grow out of it. I dun need to explain dat to you! Ha!"

"How you were 'made'? Wow, so *edgy*. You into that sort of thing?"

"Nooo! I'm not one of thoshe people!"

"Enh, that's beside the point."

Pocchi released the biceps seat belt restraining toddler Masato and patted three-year-old Amante on the head.

"Real talk, though, I think you've got a chance here specifically *because* of who you are. Same way as I acted like a fool and caused so many problems for my mom *because* she was such a big part of my life—and I just couldn't handle that. I think one day soon, you'll figure out that moms are really amazing. So don't chicken out and piss yourself, you hear?"

"Me? Pissh myshelf?! Don't be a total weirdo! Weirdo Pacchi!"

"My name ain't Pacchi—ow!"

Toddler Amante had just bitten Pocchi's arm.

When he flinched, she slithered out of his arm and ran off as fast as she could.

"Uh, hey! Amante, stop! It's too dangerous!"

"Shut up! Weirdo Picchi! Backwardsh Picchi! You even went bald backwardsh!"

"Yo, Amante! I don't care about Pucchi, but that lasht one'sh mean to everyone with a mohawk!"

"You're plenty mean yourself, Masato. Whatever—Amante! Look up! There's a monster!"

"What?"

Amante had made it to the sand, but she stopped in her tracks, looking up.

A child-sized starfish was falling toward her, spinning. It was about to hit!

Then...

"Amante!"

"......Huh?"

Hahako had her arms around toddler Amante. She'd cast aside her weapons and thrown both arms around her protectively.

Three-year-old Amante had her face in Hahako's chest and couldn't see anything...but she felt Hahako's body shake.

"Oh dear! That went in deep! We'd better treat her fast!"

"Hahako! I'm gonna pull it out! Grit your teeth—here goes!"

"I'll heal it! Don't move. *Spara la magia per mirare... Cura!*"

"Wait, what's going on? The spell activated but the wound isn't closing! Hang on, this isn't some weird thing like Hahako is immune to healing spells because she's a unique being, is it?"

Toddler Amante could clearly hear the panic in their voices.

She knew things were bad, really bad. But...

"Amante, are you okay? You aren't hurt, are you?"

Hahako pulled back, Amante's well-being her only concern. Checking her over for injuries, she even brushed the sand off Amante's feet as if it were the most urgent thing in her life.

"W-wait! Hahako, calm down!" Amante said. "You're in worshe shape den me—!"

"I'm fine! I just forgot to guard and damaged the core of my very being, but that's all!"

"Dat shounds like a very big deal?! Are you gonna shtop exishting?!"

"Healing spells may not work, but there are repair programs, so it's probably fine."

"Pwobably?!"

"What matters is that you're all right, Amante. Tell me if anything hurts!"

"Argh! I'm fine, okay? I'm not the leasht bit hurt! Shee?"

Toddler Amante waved her arms around, showing how healthy she was. "Oh, good!" "Hngg?!" And she was quickly hugged very tight.

Around them, the battle was drawing to a close.

The starfish that had wounded Hahako had fled, regrouped with a few limp companions, and formed a giant starfish again.

Immediately afterward, Mamako's full-powered attacks took it down. At last it was defeated, leaving only a giant gold star behind. The final decorative item.

The evacuees cheered. The mothers-at-arms breathed a sigh of relief.

"How do we take this with us?" "I think I can get it in my bag!" "Nah, no way it'll fit." "If we fold it…?" The girls swiftly faced another dire problem.

Meanwhile…

"……"

"……"

Hahako gently released toddler Amante. For a long moment, they each stared wordlessly at the ground.

Hahako had hugged Amante, fully aware she would be rejected. And Amante had been saved despite all her resistance. Neither seemed to know what to say next.

Seeing them getting nowhere, toddler Masato came over and bonked Amante on the head.

"Yo, Amante. There'sh only one ting you shay here."

"Wh-what'sh dat?"

"It'sh obvioush! Don't overthink it. Jusht shay da firsht ting dat comesh to mind."

He gave her a little push. She stumbled but then took a step toward Hahako.

There was a long internal battle. Mamako, toddler Masato, Pocchi, and Pocchi's mom all watched over her. Amante's fingers twitched; her toes drew lines in the sand…

And then she finally reached out and grabbed Hahako's dress, tugging on it.

"…………………Thank you."

Her lips were pouting, and she was sulking a bit…but she got the words out.

Hahako said nothing. She just nodded and wiped the tears from her eyes.

"Argh! Arghhhh! Arghhhhh! Masato Oosuki!" *Bonk bonk bonk bonk!*

"Ow! Wh-why are you hitting me? Shtop!"

Just covering her embarrassment. *Bonk bonk bonk bonk.* Red all the way to her ears and taking it out on him. Everyone just watched, smiling. "…Urgh…" "M-M-M-Ma-kun?!" Since he was toddlerized, Masato had very little HP and was soon down for the count.

Three-year-old Amante leveled up.

Somehow, they managed to get the gold star into Porta's shoulder bag and made their retreat.

At the exit to Thermo, the Mom Guild members gathered, seeing the heroic party off.

"You're leaving already? It wouldn't hurt to take a breather."

"We do have urgent business... Oh, I know! Your net fishing event might have been canceled, but I know a delightful event that's happening instead! You should look forward to that."

"Oh? What could that be? If you say it's delightful, Mamako, I'm sure something genuinely incredible will happen. We'll all look forward to *that*! See you again."

"Yes, I wish you all the best of fortunes. Come on, Ma-kun."

"Ugh...f-fine! But just for today!"

He held Mommy's hand so he wouldn't fall down.

So did the other group.

"I'll let you hold her haaaand, Amaaaante. I'm da big shiiiiishter."

"Amante, ya gotta show it. In body language."

"I—I know! Humph!"

Toddler Sorella held a white hand. Toddler Fratello held the left hand. And toddler Amante took the right. All three were holding hands with Hahako.

The beach fight had left everyone covered in sand, but they'd cleaned themselves off and were ready—

"Oh, hang on. We have some fresh seaweed here; would you like some? It's perfect for wrapping onigiri! The children would love that."

""Oh, are you sure?""

Mamako and Hahako stopped. "What about some fried mackerel?" "Perfect for breakfast!" "I've got some whitefish..." "Oh, those look good!" More and more offers of gifts, all of them irresistible to a mother.

This was dangerous.

"If you could just wait a moment, I'll run and fetch them! Won't be a minute!"

"I suppose a minute won't be—"

"Wait, wait! Hey, Mommy! Aren't we in a hurry?"

"Oh, that's right. We are...we *are*, but..."

The irresistible lure of idle chatter, the ultimate pleasure for a mom!

Pocchi's mother was not about to let this opportunity pass her by! Her smile broadened.

As she searched for a topic, any topic, a topic strong enough to stop Mamako in her tracks…her eyes locked on to three-year-old Masato and the three toddler Kings.

"Oh, right. Have they had all their shots? There's a pediatrician's office right down the road from here."

"""""Eep?!"""""

"They had…wait, have they? They're about three now. I think they're due for a Japanese encephalitis shot!"

"There's a standard schedule in your MCH handbook. There are two shots for three-year-olds, with a bit of a gap in between. You've got to make sure they're taken care of."

"""""Augh?!"""""

More needles. More doctors. "But I refushe!" The toddlers reflectively tried to escape, but Mamako and Hahako took their hands firmly, not letting it happen.

"No, no, no, noooo! No more shoooootsh!" *Flail.*

"Mah worsht memoriesh, dredged up again!" *Tremble.*

"We're children! We feel da pain sho much more intenshly! And you wanna inflict dat on ush again? Never! Masato Oosuki, do shomething!"

"Argh, you leave me with no choice! C'mon!"

The terrible three-year-olds prepared for war!

The ultimate attack of cornered children!

"""""WAHHHHHHHHHHHHHHHHHHHHHHHHHHHHHHHHHHH-HHHHHHHHHHHHH!"""""

They exploded with sobs. "Crap, that's loud!" The older girls covered their ears, even closed their eyes! It was very unpleasant!

Heh-heh-heh…nothing can defeat a crying child! Victory is ours!

In the face of this ultimate attack, even Mamako and Hahako would be forced to surrender, to respect their children's wishes…

""Okay, here we go!"" They smiled.

"""""It's ineffective?!"""""

If it was for their children's own good, mothers could harden their hearts, ignore any selfish behavior, and haul them right to the clinic. Mothers were strong like that.

"M-Mamako, we'll just kill some time nearby," said Wise.

"Let's agree to meet up at the giant fir later," added Medhi.

"Yes, that should be fine. Enjoy yourselves!"

"Good luck, little ones! I'll be rooting for you from very far away!" cheered Porta.

"…Me too," Mone said. She was acting oddly quiet, but she followed after Wise, Medhi, and Porta.

Hypodermic time.

The toddlers had been dragged off to the pediatrician's office. Their crying was no longer audible.

The girls were walking on the deserted shore, sighing with relief.

"How can Mamako and Hahako stand all that? That's a real feat."

"I think they're really great! I respect them!"

"I can only hope we're capable of that someday. But what do we do now?"

"Mm…I'm not all that hungry, so I guess we could look at clothes? If you've got any better ideas, I'm up for anything. Huh?"

When Wise looked around the group, she noticed someone missing.

Mone was way at the back, both hands clutching her chest.

"Yo, Mone, what's up?"

"Mone? Is something wrong?"

"I'm afraid so…looking at Masato and those girls…I just really wanted someone to hold my hand. I really needed a hug. I got really jealous and wanted someone to spoil me…maybe that's why."

Mone smiled apologetically and looked down at the hands on her chest.

They were covering a hole. A hole in her chest, like a bottomless pit—nothing visible within those depths.

"Augh, what the hell is that? What's going on?! Eep!"

"I don't really know, myself. It's like a wind blowing through my heart…if I don't fill it with something, something bad's gonna happen. What do we do?"

"I—I know! I'll get something to fill it!"

"Porta? Wait! If you get too close…"

Too late.

When Porta stepped closer to Mone, she was lifted up. "Whoa?!" A moment later, her body was sucked into the hole, and she was gone.

"Porta?! Holy crap!"

"I was afraid of that…I can't hold back the craving. What do we do?"

"That's what we want to know! How do we stop it? How can we help?"

"Help? …Um, well…maybe if the two of you spoil me…"

Mone's eyes looked up at them, turning hollow.

And Wise and Medhi were sucked into the hole in her chest so fast, they could not even scream.

"Huh? Where'd they go? I'm all alone…so lonely…someone spoil me, please…"

Mone leaned forward, staring into the hole in her chest.

And then Mone herself was sucked into it, vanishing into thin air.

A Christmas Memory

Medhi

Masato, do you have any Christmas memories?

Dah.

Masato

Mamako

He's a baby, so he can't talk! Tee-hee!
What about you, Medhi?

I usually went to see a light show with
my mother. She said beautiful sights
foster a keen sense of aesthetics.

Medhi

Wise

Yet somehow you got all dark
and twisted insi—owww!!!

Whoa! Here, Wise, this potion
helps heal stomped feet!

Porta

MERRY CHRISTMAS, MEDHI

Chapter 3 Children Spend Their Lives Locked in Combat with Fun. Childhood Is a Battle Royale.

The trees around the giant fir stretched out their branches, creating platforms like the scaffolding on a construction site.

"Wow...we're so high up!"

"Hey! Masato Oosuki! Don't make it rock!"

"I ain't scared at all! Heights don't bother me!" Fratello said, shaking like a leaf.

Picking their way gingerly across these platforms were three children, now grown to around ten years old. They'd listened to their mothers, held their hands, and survived the painful shots. These results had led to their recognition as good children.

They'd been given new outfits to match their new sizes and were wearing warm work clothes over those, with safety helmets. It was scary up here, but the work was fun, too. They had treasure chests, jewels, bells—all kinds of ornaments to hang from the fir branches.

"Yo, Sorella, can you handle that one?"

"Sure, suuuuure. Got iiiiit."

Child Sorella was totally fine with heights. She'd grown enough to equip her giant tome, so she was riding that around, hanging tinsel, wrapping it around and around the branches.

Tree trimming was proceeding smoothly.

"Looking good, everyone. We should have no problems starting the Christmas event."

Shiraaase had a helmet on and was serving as the foreman. She looked up at the increasingly resplendent giant fir and nodded with approval. Mamako and Hahako were beside themselves with worry, afraid their children would fall.

"But should we just have started without them like this? The girls still aren't back…"

"I suppose they're still enjoying Thermo. We should have specified a time to regroup."

"They'll just have to accept that it's their fault for showing up late. The schedule demands that we work while we still can. If we don't start on time, parents the world over will be in trouble."

"Trouble? Well, I suppose it is Christmas. Decorating the house and doing all that cooking just takes so much time."

"And then there's this," Dark-Mom Deathmother said, emerging from the snow hut with a white bag in her arms.

Using her body to hide it from the children above, she opened the bag. Inside were three small boxes, one wrapped adorably in a pink ribbon, one in elegant paper and a blue ribbon, and one sloppily wrapped in newspaper and red tape.

"Oh, yes. We have to get presents ready!"

"One is from me. The other two are from Kazuno and Medhimama. I won't say which is which."

"It was a sudden request, but they both agreed immediately. One pretended she didn't like the idea, but…"

"Tee-hee. I can imagine who. But we'll have to do the same! This is a mother's duty."

"A mother's duty…" Hahako looked grave. She gulped.

"I wish I could tell you to relax…but this is a Christmas present. It's undeniable that your reputation as a parent depends upon it."

"It pains me to say that this will be the first Christmas that Porta and I have spent together as a family. I threw everything I had into this present, trying to make up for all the loneliness I've caused her. So…Hahako, it's your time to step up, too."

"Yes, of course. I *will* be those girls' mother. I'll find the right gifts to make them happy even if I have to search the world! Even if I have to make a new world!"

"Hahako, you don't want to spoil them *too* much. Tee-hee."

Mamako smiled, talking her down.

"Hey! Grown-ups! What are you hiding?"

"I bet I can guess, but we're done up here!"

"Mm. Job done."

"All the tinsel's huuuung. Unless you see anywhere that needs moooore?"

The tree decorations were, indeed, complete. The ornament at the top was still missing, but the giant fir was beautifully decorated, and glittered magnificently.

Shiraaase did a lap around the tree, inspecting it, and gave it the seal of approval.

"Then let's get started. Eyes up, everyone!"

She rapped her knuckles against the trunk. As the kids gathered around the base of the tree, a warm light emerged from within.

The tree's glow lit up their surroundings and beyond, sending a message of joy to all corners of the world.

A brief squeal, like a mild ringing in the ears.

Across Catharn, grown-up NPCs turned to look at the sky.

"Is that... Oh, I get it."

All of them understood immediately.

The capital was covered in clouds, which soon began dropping white crystals.

"Mommy! Look! Snow! So weird!"

"Yes...you don't usually get surprise snow. It's getting cold! Let's go inside. We need to put some warmer things on!"

The children had not yet picked up on the change. And the adults were letting them remain oblivious. It was best if they didn't know.

Wouldn't want to ruin it for them. While the children all frolicked in the snow, the adults exchanged tense glances.

Secret celebration prep was underway.

Even in the merchant city Yomamaburg, which stood in the center of the wastelands...

"A presentation worthy of the holy night is required. Snow will not fall here, but we must make our own snow. Adjust the hologram at once! We do have some time left, but that's no reason to dillydally!"

"Manager! The outfits are done! We'll need people to try them on…"

"Well done. This way."

In the city's largest casino, the manager stopped barking orders, smiled as warmly as Santa himself, and headed to his office.

Meanwhile, in Meema, home of the Matriarchal Arts Tournament…

"Meema hosts a parade of guards in costume every year! The children are looking forward to it! We must make it a success!"

"Then you'd better get cracking. I'll mind the guard station for you. You guards go get ready for the parade!"

"That would help a lot. We'll take you up on that offer. Come on, men! Hop to it!"

"What?" "Mommy, what's happening?" "I don't get it!" "Hugs!" "Hugs!"

"You don't need to get it yet. It'll be more fun later."

The guards all followed the captain out. Growlette watched them go, shielding her kids from the frigid winds.

And in the coastal town of Thermo…

"Pocchi, I don't mean anything by this, but could you wait here in the Mom Guild? I've got some urgent business."

"Wait, Mom, I know what this is. Yeah, I'm your kid, but I'm also a childcare worker at the Mom Guild nursery, which means I'm like a dad to these kids."

"Oh…heh-heh-heh. You certainly have grown! That's a little sad, but Mom's happy for you. Okay, Pocchi! Let's make this a good one."

"Yeah! The Thermo winter specialty—we'll make it the best one yet! Come on, boys!"

"""Yeah!"""

Pocchi and the brutish childcare workers shouldered bundles of cables and raced off toward the tower dungeon. Their mothers and the setting sun watched them go.

The world was getting ready for Christmas.

*   *   *

"…Yeah, that'll do."

The snow hut had been cleared away and new furnishings installed near the base of the giant fir tree.

At the venue was a massive banquet table covered in elegant candelabras, and a brick fireplace was nearby. There were also enough comfortable couches to seat everyone. Dark-Mom Deathmother was seated on one of them, tapping and swiping away on her tablet. Her participation was strictly voluntary.

The style was reminiscent of Christmas parties in Northern Europe. Truly a scene that promised a most wonderful time…

"Heh, it's perfect. Well, Masato? Have I impressed you yet?"

"Sure, Shiraaase, it's 'perfect.' Except for the fact that there's no ceiling or walls."

"An intentional oversight to allow you to soak in the splendor of the locale. We have snow wards installed, never fear. And there's one other feature to ensure the party is a success."

Shiraaase pointed behind the giant fir.

A figure in red appeared.

"Ma-kun! I tried it on, but what do you think? It's Santa Mommy! Mommy Santa! Hee-hee."

Mamako was wearing a red-and-white Santa costume so skimpy, she seemed ready to spill out of it.

A vein throbbed on Masato's face, but he forced himself to smile pleasantly.

"Uh, sure, it looks great. Totally."

"Oh my! Ma-kun's doing the calm before the storm."

"Here you are, doing everything you can to make this a fun event, and he's radiating hostility. You've got a lot of nerve, Masato."

"It's a normal reaction! Nobody my age would welcome their mother dressed as Santa…gasp!"

The giant fir was glowing with the light of punishment. Naughty children who dissed their mom's cosplay would need to be reformed, starting over from the very—

"No, no, no, I didn't mean that! I was just kidding!" His desperate pleas managed to talk it down.

"Th-the costume itself isn't a problem! It's just, uh...yeah, cooking! I just figured that if you've got a lot of cooking to do today, a different outfit would be more practical!"

"Oh, that's right! We'll have to start cooking soon or we won't be ready in time for dinner! I'd like to prep tomorrow's dishes while I'm at it. Hahako!"

"Yes, let's make this the best meal yet."

"Er, but if you could just change first... Nobody's listening."

The two moms ran into the kitchen that had been set up for this party venue. They were inspecting the available ingredients, formulating a plan of attack.

Clearly Christmas prep was going smoothly.

"So the moms are cooking... And what are you good little boys and girls doing?"

"I'm gonna do my best to ignore what she's wearing, and help cook. If that helps me get designated as a good kid and grow more, all the better. Right, Amante?"

"I won't! I'd never help a mother cook! Humph!"

"Oh, really? You and Hahako were getting along so well. Yo, Sorella, Fratello, what's going on?"

"I dunnoooo. But I agree with Amante heeeere."

"Mm. Ain't about to help no moms."

"All of you, huh? What gives? You holding a grudge about the shots or something? That can't be true, right?"

The little Kings all rubbed their arms where the needles had poked them, avoiding his gaze.

Cleeeeeeearly holding a grudge.

"Sheesh, don't be so childish. I guess you *are* children, but..."

"Three steps forward, two steps back. That's how bonds are made. How about we make a different task for the child team? This way."

Shiraaase pointed, and a door festooned with Christmas decorations appeared out of nowhere.

When it opened, there was a toy store inside. Its name? Hello Mama Toys.

Robots, dolls, stuffed animals, toy cars, toy swords, princess outfits. Even toys for older kids, and real weapons, armor, and items. The store was so big, they couldn't see the far wall, and it was stuffed to the brim with enough toys to delight children of all ages.

"Wow...awesome..."

"This is the legendary toy shop that only opens on Christmas Eve, with doors appearing all over the world. Masato, Amante, Sorella, and Fratello—go explore this store!"

"Explore? Are we looking for something in particular?"

"Whatever you wish. I'm afraid you won't be able to take it with you...but perhaps Santa will bring it to you later."

"Santa...? Sorry, Shiraaase, we're too old for that..."

"Santa will bring us presents?! Then we've got to get this right!" *Excited.*

"We're good kiiiids, so he'll definitely cooooome." *Excited.*

"Mm. Gotta hang a big ole stockin'. Maybe a couple of spares." *Excited.*

Guess the girls weren't too old.

"Are they serious?"

"Masato, don't go shattering the dreams of children. Now then, everything you do in the shop will be broadcast to your parents in real time. If the presents you wish for are placed by your pillows in the morning, that's why."

"I feel like you've just destroyed more dreams than I ever could, but okay."

"Why are you still talking to *her*?! Masato Oosuki, let's go!"

"Gah?!"

Little Amante was clearly done waiting, and she grabbed child Masato by the collar, hauling him bodily into the toy store.

Santa Mamako and Hahako watched them go, a little worried.

"Ma-kun! Mommy wants to go with you, but I'm just too busy! Be a good boy in the store, okay? Look after the girls."

"Got it! Leave them to me!"

"Humph. No way Masato Oosuki could ever look after me! Hahako, we're going in."

"Yes. Have a good time. Be nice to everyone!"

With their mother's approval, it was time for the children's adventure.

The shelves were packed with toys. The aisles were packed with children and teenagers. "I want this!" "And this!" All having the time of their lives. Squeals and laughter echoing through the store.

As Masato and the little Kings made their way down the main passage, a five-year-old boy tripped and fell. But he was in too big a rush to stop and cry. He got right back up and ran off smiling.

"This place is so chaotic, it's making my head hurt. I mean, I'm excited, too, but...even if our bodies are children, our minds are all grown up. We can stay calm—"

"What are those things over there?! I'm gonna go see!" *Dash.*

"Yo, Amante, don't run off alone! You'll get lost!"

"They've got magical girl costuuuumes! So cuuuute! I wonder if there are any necromanceeeeers?!"

"Not you, too, Sorella?! Aren't you already a necromancer? Why do you need a costume?!"

"Sonny—I can't hold it in no longer." Fratello was trembling.

"Fratello, seriously? Argh, go before we come in! Fine, I'll help find the bathroom, just hold it a little longer."

Not only could Masato not relax and look around, but he couldn't even take two steps. "How do parents do it?" He had a lot of sympathy for anyone looking after little kids suddenly. But he was forced to play the role here.

First, the call of nature.

Once Fratello's bladder was empty, they came back to the main shop...

"Mm? Is that...?"

…and found a girl wearing reindeer antlers. With a large shoulder bag. A very cute reindeer girl.

Two mascots dangling from her bag, Piita and the slightly larger Piitamama. Which meant this was definitely…

"Yo, Porta!"

"Huh? …Oh, Masato! And the Kings?"

When she turned around, it was definitely Porta.

"Welcome! This is Hello Mama Toys!"

"Thanks, good to be here…wait, why are you welcoming us?"

"I work here now!"

"Why would you be…uh, come to think of it, they did say doors opened all over the world. Did you come here from Thermo?"

"Yes! I did!"

"And you saw how busy the place was and volunteered to help out? Yeah, that's just like you. You're such a good girl! We were worried when you never showed up, but this explains it."

"Sorry to worry you! I'm just fine!"

Reindeer Porta was all smiles.

But she was shaking her head really hard.

"Mm? What's wrong? Are you denying that?"

"No, not denying anything! I'm fine!" *Shake shake.*

"Then why are you shaking your head? What's that mean?"

"You're imagining it!" *Shake shake.*

"No, no, that doesn't make sense. What's got into you, Porta?"

He put his hands on her soft cheeks, stopping the shaking. It stopped. "Are you okay?" "Yes!" She seemed okay.

But the moment he let go, she started shaking her head again, still smiling.

Child Masato frowned, puzzled.

"Porta, there you are. We were looking for you."

"We finally found—oh, Masato! And the Kings! You guys sure got big while we weren't looking. Kids grow up so fast!"

"Oh, it's Medhi, and…who's the lady talking like she's somebody's long-lost aunt?"

Two more familiar faces came darting over, expertly weaving through the throngs of other children.

The first was wearing a cape decked out like a Christmas tree, covered in ornaments. Medhi, dressed as a tree.

The other had her arms and legs sticking out of a papier-mâché sled. Perhaps it would be best not to meet her eye.

"Medhi, who is that?"

"No clue whatsoever."

"It's me! Wise! I wanna gripe about this costume more than anyone! But it's my job! This comes with the territory!"

"R-right, okay. How noble of you. So you're both working here, too?"

"Yep. Voluntarily helping out."

"Yes, of our own free will."

Sled Wise and Tree Medhi both proudly shook their heads.

"Uh-huh. I appreciate your candor. I take it you're actually just after the wages, then?"

"No, we're n—y-yes, exactly!" *Shake shake.*

"Not quite tr—totally true! Right you are!" *Shake shake.*

"Wait, which is it? Stop shaking your heads!"

"We'd like to—but nope! That's our job!" *Shake shake.*

"Don't be si—r-right! Our job!" *Shake shake.*

"How is that your job?"

They both sounded like they always did, but their actions weren't quite adding up.

Sled Wise, Tree Medhi, and Reindeer Porta were all shaking their heads, waving their arms and legs around cryptically, but smiling brightly the whole time.

That was weird.

"Masato Oosuki! No time to stop and chat! We've got to pick the presents Santa will bring us! Come on!"

"Yo, Amante, stop pulling me. These three are acting weird…"

"Don't worry about us! You kids focus on your presents." *Shake shake.*

"Children have gathered from all over the world, and the shop is very crowded. If you don't hurry, you might not have much of a selection left!" *Shake shake.*

"That would be baaaaad! Let's get moviiiing!"

"Mm. Strike while the iron's hot."

"If you want to know more about anything in the store, just ask! I'll explain it! Masato, this way!" *Shake shake.*

"R-right..."

It was bugging him, but the three child Kings raced off excitedly. Wise's sled runners were poking him in the back.

"Quit pushing! By the way, where's Mone? Is she here, too?"

"She's around somewhere. She's fine! Go on!" *Shake shake.*

"Okay, I'm moving. How are you shaking your head and pushing me at the same time?"

Seemed like his only option was to explore the shop awhile.

The children started walking—and only took a few steps before... "What's that?!" "Don't run off!" No force could contend with an unrestrained child. So excited, so carefree.

But behind them...

Argh, why can't we communicate? What is this?!

It's bad is what it is. We might slip further under her control...

Urp...I think I'm already losing...

Inside the girls' heads, they were screaming.

Quit looking for presents and focus on us!

Do something quick before there aren't any presents left to choose, Masato!

I have more important things to explain than our product line, Masato!

They had urgent news to tell him, but whenever they tried to speak, something else came out.

They had to try and communicate physically, but that was not proving effective.

Masato, notice! Right there! Below you! The real bad thing!

Sled Wise stared at her feet, willing him to look. It did not work.

*　　*　　*

The basement below the toy shop was where the stock was managed.

When kids picked out what they wanted, that info was broadcast live to their parents. And if the item was purchased, the orders would come in here, and the workers would spring into action.

Magical hands would pick up the items sold, quickly wrap them, and drop them down the one-way chute in the floor to a transport circle. In the blink of an eye, the present would be in the parents' hands.

It was all unmanned and automated, moving swiftly and steadily.

Not one person here.

"…Begging for them…spoiling them by buying them…it's a special day, so you're extra spoiled, with lots of presents, that's nice. Buy more. Buy more and more."

No humans were present, but there was one being busy awakening to her powers as Dark God. She was floating in the air, muttering to herself.

"…Not enough spoiling out there. Wise, Medhi, Porta, stop resisting. Help me. I'll lend you my power…"

Her hands reached toward the floor above, releasing a sweet scent, like condensed milk.

"Masato Oosuki. How about this? State your opinion."

"Uh…sure, why not?"

"What kind of a response is that? Take this seriously!"

"Seriously, how?"

Child Amante was busy showing him a tiger-striped jacket. Most people would probably see it as the sort of thing a frumpy lady from Osaka would wear. If he was honest, Amante would hit him.

Maybe the staff could help…but the cosplay teens were swarmed with other kids, completely preoccupied. No getting anywhere near them. Couldn't investigate their weird behavior, either.

Oh well. Time to man up.

"I think it looks great," he said, smiling.

"There's no way it looks great! I should never have asked you, Masato Oosuki. You're not ready."

Apparently, it had been a test. Girls were terrifying. Child Amante turned her back and stalked off back toward the shelves.

They were in the adventurer gear section. Even if their bodies were kids, their minds were still in high school. Toys didn't hold much appeal. Being given a toy would probably make them want to cry.

Child Sorella and child Fratello were also looking to improve their loadouts and combing through everything on offer.

"Mm...they don't have much in my styyyyle..."

"Men's clothes are all too big! None of this is gonna fit me. But I ain't never gonna wear kid clothes! This is a tough one..."

"Ohh, a tiger-striped string bikiniiiii...Amanteeee! Fancy thiiiis?"

"Mm. That's one for her."

"Are you both completely stupid? We're picking presents here! What kind of parents would give their kid something like—I mean, Santa's giving us these, and he doesn't give bikinis!"

She seemed to believe she'd walked back her statement in time...

But little Masato heard her loud and clear.

"...So, Amante, you do know better."

"Wh-what on earth are you talking about? Even if I did know that Christmas presents are given by your parents and not Santa, I wouldn't say it out loud!"

"Yeah, still honest to a fault. You're just doing the Santa thing because you've got no idea how to handle getting a present from Hahako, right? You're running away."

Child Amante's smile froze. She was an open book.

"I—I am not! I would never run from a mother! I am she who rejects the concept of mothers, Anti-Mom Amante! So long as mothers exist, I will resist to the bitter end!"

"Yeah, time to stop resisting and face the music."

Masato shook his head, expecting her to wheel around and yell at him. But instead, Amante just sighed.

"...I wish it were that easy. But I was *made* to rebel. As long as that's part of me, I can't ever be someone's kid. But if that part of me were removed, I wouldn't be me anymore. So what am I supposed to do?"

"Well..."

Good question. He didn't have an answer. Child Masato couldn't think of anything to say.

Then...

"That's easy! Just go get spoiled." Sled Wise came sliding in with a blunt order.

"Have faith in the power of spoiling," Tree Medhi said, like she was spreading gospel. "Spoiling is the salvation of all things. Lost children—go forth, and be spoiled."

Finally Porta came dashing in with a cheery show of support. "Spoiling makes children and mommies happy!"

"Um...what's gotten into you guys?"

"Everyone rebels against their parents sometimes. I sure did! Even if you want to stop, sometimes you can't help yourself."

"But that's nothing to worry about. There's a simple technique that will resolve all your problems. Spoiling. Just let her put her arms around you, let her accept you for you who are, and give yourself over to the beautiful spoils of love."

"If children want to be spoiled, mommies are very happy! My mommy was! This is anecdotal, based on my own personal experience, but that makes it true! So..."

If you order in the next three minutes, you'll get a special discount! Call the number on your screen! Act now! ...was definitely the vibe they had going.

There was a sweet scent in the air over their presentation. This was suspicious.

"Ummm...have these giiiiirls...gone completely craaaazy?"

"Mm. Y'all were weird before, but now yer downright loonies. What do ya make of it, sonny?"

"Yeah. I mean, what they're *saying* isn't wrong, but doing a hard sell on spoiling is definitely odd... Hey, are you all—"

"Wait! There's something behind them!" child Amante yelled. She grabbed a short sword from the rack nearby and threw it in Sled Wise's direction.

The blade brushed past her neck, pierced the shadow behind her, and embedded itself in the shelf beyond.

And affixed to the tip of that blade...was what looked like an oversized spider.

Its thin legs thrashed a few times, and then it faded away.

"The hell is that thing?"

"It was clinging to Wise the Sage's back and was stabbing her with its needlelike mouth. Since no gems dropped, that wasn't technically a monster. Perhaps it was a fairy or the like?"

"If it looks like a bug, I don't really wanna call it a fairy, but... Wise, are you okay now—yikes?!"

A second spider fairy was peering around Sled Wise's shoulder. She certainly didn't seem to be okay.

And there were more on Tree Medhi and Reindeer Porta's shoulders. They were injecting some sort of fluid into the girls, who were now moving closer with eerie smiles on their faces.

"Amante, here I am telling you all about the wonders of spoiling, and you react like that? What's your problem?"

"You leave us with no choice. If you refuse to understand our message, we'll have to beat some manners into you."

"Yes! I think proper education is best! I'll help!"

The three girls all struck fighting poses. Even Reindeer Porta took her mascot doll, Piita, off her shoulder bag, and it grew until it was six feet tall.

The spider fairies turned into syringes, which the girls and doll armed themselves with.

Time for combat.

"Yo! Are we seriously gonna fight brainwashed party members? And if we lose, we get injected?!"

"This is really happening! We've got to fight back!"

"Now, now, are you sure about that? We're the Christmas costume girls, beloved by children everywhere."

"Gather around, children," Tree Medhi said, smiling broadly. "If you don't do as we say, you'll be going on the naughty list. Make sure you back us up!"

Children came rushing in from all around. "You can do it!" "Go, girls!" "Beat the naughty kids!" Like they were watching a stunt show. This was gonna be rough.

"We're not the bad kiiiids! You're so meeeean! I've grown up a bit and can use some maaaagic. Maybe I should just take everyone oooout."

"Yeah, blow 'em all away!"

"Wait, wait, wait, do not under any circumstances attack the kids in the crowd!"

"Right," Amante said. "Doesn't look like those kids have fairies on them. These three are the only ones being mind-controlled."

"Right, riiiiiight. Then Wiiiiiise, Medhiiiii, and Porta's doll Piiiiiita. Those are our taaaargets."

"Tch, fine, we'll do it yer way."

Child Sorella raised her hands, and a giant tome appeared above her head. Child Amante began quietly chanting a spell. Their magic was going to be the key to this battle.

The children's toy shop battle began!

"Heh-heh! This is the perfect chance to pay you back for everything you've done! The punishment you've had—"

"*Tacere!*" Child Amante's silence spell interrupted Wise.

Sled Wise's magic was sealed. Tree Medhi's magic was sealed. Reindeer Porta and Piita were unaffected.

"At least let me finish! Argh, I hate you!"

"This sort of thing is supposed to be Wise's specialty…" Medhi hung her head.

"Don't worry! I have items to fix magic seals! I'll get them out right away!"

"Yeah, with Porta, they'll recover quick…but I bought us some time! Everyone, spread out! Guerrilla tactics!"

The team of children nodded, and each ran off in a different direction.

Masato ran headlong down the shop's lengthy aisles.

"I've gotta find something that'll work as a weapon…oh! That should do it!"

Masato found a toy bazooka that fired sponge bullets. He immediately equipped it.

Then he peered around the corner of a shelf, like a hunter (despite being the one pursued). Where had Sled Wise and Tree Medhi gone? "Oh, there!" "He's over here!" "Gah!" Random children saw him and started yelling. He beat a hasty retreat.

"Argh, do you think we're playing hide-and-seek?! Knock it off, this isn't a game!"

This was a serious fight. "Oh, armor!" Child Masato quickly equipped the transforming superhero belt and ran down the aisle.

It wasn't clear if the transformation belt would actually function as armor, but like villagers always say, if you don't equip it, there's no point!

The four members of the kid team had to do battle with the three costumed teens.

We've got the advantage of numbers, but they're far stronger…which means…

They had to gang up and take them out one at a time. He had to gather equipment and meet up with the rest of his team.

Where had the three little Kings gone? Child Masato poked his head out in the main aisle, looking for them.

"Aughhh! They found meeee! Whyyyy?!"

"Isn't it obvious? The giant magic tome floating over your head is a dead giveaway."

"We're gonna give you all shots together! For now, behave."

Child Sorella had been captured by Sled Wise and Tree Medhi.

"That idiot…"

The kid team was already down one member.

Then...

"There you are, Masato Oosuki!"

"Whoa, that sounds like Amante...but isn't?!"

Someone had tapped his shoulder, but when he turned around, he found Mamako's smiling face! On closer inspection, it *was* Amante, wearing a Mamako mask.

"D-don't scare me like that! Where'd you even find that thing?"

"In the face armor section. Equipping everything you find is the key to any battle royale, so I went ahead and put it on, but...they make merch of her now? Just who is your mom becoming?"

"Don't ask me. Anyway, I'm glad we met up. We're gonna have to work together. You in?"

"We don't exactly have a choice, so yeah."

Child Amante nodded firmly. In her hands was a Mom-Idol-branded microphone.

"...Is that a weapon?" "If you press the button, music comes out." Didn't seem like it would do much damage.

Time to move. One eye on the throngs of children around them. Carefully.

"We just need Fratello...think she's nearby?"

"She should be around here somewhere. Fratello's quicker than Sorella, so she should be harder to catch..."

"*Mahhh...leggoooooooo...*"

"Yeah, I think that's a no."

Hiding behind a promo sign, they took a quick look. Yep.

Child Fratello had found a very manly, badly damaged martial artist costume, but was currently held tightly in giant Piita's arms. So was child Sorella.

Right by the shop entrance.

"We're sunk..."

"Yeah, if they hold them there, they're also blocking the escape route. I had a plan B involving running out of the shop and calling in the moms to help but...that's no longer an option."

The two of them would have to fight. Knowing the odds were against them. They'd have to grit their teeth and form a plan...

But as he racked his brain, a Mamako mask was thrust out toward him.

"...What?"

"Why not ask? We're talking about Mamako Oosuki here. Even if you don't speak directly to her, she might just notice and handle the situation. Maybe."

"Mm...well, yeah, with my mom, that is possible..."

"Then go on. Let your mom spoil you."

"Spoil?"

"What Wise the Sage said wasn't *that* off base, was it? You said so yourself. And she said when we're stuck, it's okay to let our moms spoil us."

"Yeah, I agree to an extent, but still..."

"Then show me how it's done, Masato Oosuki. Or are you telling me to do something you can't even do yourself? Really?"

She didn't seem to be mocking him. Child Amante seemed serious.

It seemed like she was looking for a solid basis to answer the conflict raging within herself.

I've gotta let Mom spoil me? Seriously? Ugh, this is rough...

Little Masato wanted to help Amante out. He did, but...

But for an adolescent boy to just go get himself spoiled simply because someone told him to was a bit of a tall order.

But then he realized...

Oh...I guess that's exactly her *problem.*

The thing he was stuck on was hard to explain. It was just a nebulous reluctance.

And that was the same thing the Heavenly Kings were struggling with.

If he could overcome this, he could tell them anything he liked, and be proud of it. He could communicate what really mattered.

So child Masato looked the Mamako mask in the eye.

"This is gonna be rough, but you leave me no choice. Here goes nothing! Mom—"

Instantly, the gentle notes of a xylophone echoed through the store. From the PA system.

"Everyone, it's snack time! Wash your hands, then come on by!"

Mamako's voice. "…That was fast…" Before her beloved son could even ask, she was already on the move, responding with uncanny timing.

The mom skill **A Mother's Snacks** activated. "Where do we wash our hands?" "In the bathrooms!" The children all rushed off, headed for the bathrooms at the back.

The stampede of children swept Sled Wise and Tree Medhi up in it.

"Hey! There's too many! I can't move!"

"Now we can't tell where Masato and Amante are!"

Perfect.

"Nice assist, Mom! Now's our chance! Come on, Amante!"

"I'm not completely convinced, but I'm not about to blow this opportunity, either!"

Hiding in the crowds, little Masato and little Amante moved stealthily.

First, Masato attacked. He held up the sponge bazooka, taking aim…

And found two butts, coincidentally lined up right where he could easily target them. *Bam, bam.*

"Eep! Wh-what was that?!"

"Who did that?! That's inappropriate!"

Two girls spun around, clutching their rear ends. But their assailant was already gone.

Instead, music played somewhere nearby.

"Do you hear that? Isn't that the MOM-3 song?"

"Where's it coming from… Oh, over there."

Sled Wise and Tree Medhi peered down a nearby aisle.

The toy microphone was playing music and flashing lights.

This was a trap. Their backs were wide open. Two children crept up behind them.

And right in their ears…

""WAHHHHHHHHHHHHHHHHHHHH!""

""Aiiieeeeeeeeeeeeeeeee?!""

Devastating Child Attack Number One. A scream right in the ear. Ears ringing, their eyes rolled up in their heads—and they were knocked out. **Attack complete!**

"Yes! Combination victory!"

"Only Porta left."

Now for the final battle.

"Whoa! Wise and Medhi were defeated!" Reindeer Porta yelped. She'd come to check on them.

Giant Piita was still sitting by the entrance. Child Sorella and child Fratello had a firm grip on it, pinning it in place.

"Normally, we'd be the older ones. Can't do anything rough to a younger girl."

"But right now, we're younger! So we can do whatever we want, right?"

"Er…wait, I'm the oldest? Wow! That's a first! I'm so happy!"

"Good for you! Remember, Porta, if you're happy…laugh!"

Devastating Child Attack Number Two. Relentless tickles!

Fingers assaulted her sides and the back of her neck.

"Eep! Ah-ha-ha-ha-ha-ha-ha?!" Reindeer Porta let out a strained cackle and was soon rolling on the floor. But they didn't stop! More tickling!

Ten minutes later.

"Please, no more… I give up…"

Her head slumped.

"""""Victory!"""""

The toy shop battle was over. The four victorious children gave each other high fives, celebrating.

"Only Amante and I actually did any fighting…" "Oh, doooon't…" "Say that."

They'd *all* won.

A Christmas Memory

Masato

Finally, I can contribute again. But, y'know...
it's kinda hard to ask Porta about this.

Mamako

Don't worry! She can make lots of
memories in the future. Porta, what
would you like to do on Christmas?

Porta

Um...um...I just want to spend
the whole day with my mommy!

Wise

You're such a good girl! I'm
sure that wish will come true.

Medhi

It sure will. Here comes Deathmother
dashing through the snow!

Masato

Look! She's waving an approved
paid-vacation request!

MERRY CHRISTMAS, PORTA

Chapter 4 "What Do You Mean, Spoil...Aughhh!" Said the RPG Boss. What? That Never Happened?

Child Masato, Santa Mamako, and Shiraaase were walking down the main aisle of the deserted toy store.

"Other than you still being in that Santa outfit, I'm genuinely grateful. Mom, you and Deathmother really saved us."

"I had a feeling you were in trouble, Ma-kun. But there just wasn't time to make anything, so I had to serve premade snacks... Oh, but I saved some for you! They'll have to wait for tomorrow."

"Tomorrow...? Oh, Christmas. I guess today is Christmas Eve."

"Strictly speaking, it isn't Christmas Eve yet. The fir tree decorations are still incomplete. Once the star is placed on top, we can make it Christmas Eve immediately...but first, this way."

Shiraaase stopped before an EMPLOYEES ONLY door and held up her admin ID. The door unlocked.

Up ahead was a staircase that led down. Their footsteps echoed as they nervously descended to the stock management area. Dozens of one-way lines ran across the floor, and the magic hands that selected and wrapped stock were all at a standstill.

Nothing was moving. There was nobody here.

Shiraaase stroked the shelves, empty of merchandise, looking around her.

"Seems like all the presents have been sent out to parents around the world—I mean, to Santa Claus. We don't need to worry about safe delivery. However..."

"The other matter is still a concern."

Child Masato scrambled around, searching under the shelves, at the base of the magic hands, under the stairs, anywhere he could fit, but found nothing.

Santa Mamako was standing on her tiptoes, checking all the high places. "Nothing up here, either..." "Hey! Stop that!" He'd caught an unfortunate glimpse of her Christmas panties.

"Masato, you mentioned these spider fairies, but are you sure they were spiders?"

"They vanished pretty quick, so I couldn't inspect them thoroughly, but that's what they looked like. The spider part, at least. The fairy thing was just something Amante said."

"I see, so they're definitely spiders. Interesting."

Shiraaase bent her knees, crawling around with child Masato. Checking carefully to see if any of these creatures were here.

"...Not often we see you taking things this seriously, Shiraaase."

"I feel like that's a slightly rude statement, but well...this is a serious situation. Not a matter that can be easily overlooked. It could be quite grave."

"You're right... It is Christmas, after all. And whether Hahako and the Libere Kings can become family depends on the outcome... We need to be careful and make sure nothing bad happens..."

"Spiders that enhance your desire to be spoiled...spiders...spoiders...spoilers...that's such a forced pun! I can't just dismiss it!"

"Is *that* what's bothering you?"

Masato really didn't care, but this appeared to be life or death for Shiraaase.

"Ma-kun, I can't find anything that looks like a clue."

"Me neither. I guess we'll have to talk to the girls, but..."

Child Masato and Santa Mamako looked at each other and groaned in unison.

That was easier said than done.

When the three of them got back to the giant fir, they beheld a horrific sight.

"Please! Stop! Don't be mean to Porta! Leave my adorable child alone!"

"Calm yourself. This is necessary."

Hahako had her white hands extended, physically restraining the frantic Dark-Mom Deathmother.

Porta, Wise, and Medhi lay before them. The shop costumes had been removed, but their hands were bound behind their backs, and they were placed on their knees on the snow.

None of them looked happy about this, but the three Kings were standing in front of them, all holding a mug and a spoon in each hand.

"If you don't want to suffer longer, tell us what you know," demanded child Amante. "This is your final warning."

"I told you already! If you want us to talk, you've gotta spoil us first!" shouted Wise.

"How did you three end up like thiiiiis? What haaaappened?"

"Why should I talk to people who don't even understand the benefits of spoiling?" replied Medhi.

"Porta, where'd Mone go? Spit it out," said child Fratello.

"Mone is fine! Don't worry about her!"

"*Sigh*...you leave us with no choice. Torture it is!"

Child Amante stirred the contents of the mug. She carefully scooped up a spoonful of black liquid.

"W-wait, what the heck is *that*?!"

"You're not going to poison us, are you...?!"

"Nooo! Please don't!"

No mercy. Three hands reached out, squeezed the brainwashed girls' noses, and the moment their mouths opened, in went the spoons!

""""Blehhh....so bitter...""""

Oh, did they suffer.

"What are you guys even doing?"

"See for yourself."

Masato took the proffered mug and sniffed it. Then he took a sip of the black liquid.

It was black coffee. Very grown up.

"They keep going on about how sweet spoiling is, so we're giving them something bitter! Hoping the two flavors will balance out and they'll go back to normal."

"Argh! Sweets! Give me something sweet! I don't care what! My mouth is dying!" wailed Wise.

"Sheesh, you're still going on about that? Enough already!"

"Amante, here."

Masato shoved a spoon in little Amante's mouth. "Biiiiiiiiiiiiiiiiit-ter!" Massive damage to her ten-year-old tongue. She was defeated.

Either way, he didn't like seeing his party trussed up. Masato and Dark-Mom Deathmother untied all of them.

They then handed out Christmas cupcakes Santa Mamako had made, to purify their mouths. The girls were delighted. "Spoilerifically sweet!" It seemed like they'd behave themselves as long as the sweets kept coming.

"So no improvements here. Ugh... What do we do? They were injected with something, so I think they need an antidote, but—"

"Don't be ridiculous. We don't need any antidotes! We're not poisoned at all!"

"In my opinion as a specialized healer, there's no need for an antidote."

"I also don't think we need to use recovery items!"

"And you're the three people in charge of all the party healing, so... we're at a loss."

"Don't worry! I, Shiraaase, can infooorm you that I have an idea."

Shiraaase stepped forward confidently. So confidently, it was extremely worrisome.

"We must bet on a Christmas miracle! It is Christmas, after all. A most wonderful time of year! Don't you agree? You all agree, right?"

"So you have no plan..."

"It's agreed, then. Place the last ornament and transform the giant fir into a true Christmas tree. The Christmas event will officially begin! ...Porta, would you help?"

"Yes! Christmas is a time for sweets *and* spoiling, and I'm happy to help with that!"

Her motives were unswayed, but she was cooperating. Porta opened her shoulder bag, and the sail-sized gold star shot out.

Child Sorella was in charge of placing it. They tied a rope to the star, dangling it from the giant tome, and carried it to the top of the fir.

"Masatoooo! Is this gooood? What do you thiiiink?"

"A bit to the right! A bit more! Perfect! If you just set it—"

There was a squelch, and the gold star was docked.

"That was a creepy sound…"

"Yeaaah…"

They had *not* rammed the tip of the tree up the star's butt. They'd placed it properly.

Ornaments, tinsel, and the star. The three decoration stages were done, and the giant fir became a Christmas tree.

Somewhere in the distance, they heard bells ringing in celebration.

In that moment, the world officially welcomed Christmas Eve.

The sun set, night fell, and lights brighter than the stars flickered to life all across the ground.

These lights were Christmas trees. Radiating out from the giant fir, across the Motherest Mountains, all trees transformed into Christmas trees.

Lighting up in all kinds of colors, from the highest peaks to the valleys below, across the world, spreading farther and farther.

"Wow…I figured Christmas was just for kids, but if you go all out like this, it *is* pretty impressive."

"We're just getting started. The Christmas event has only just begun. Now, let's go demand a miracle or two or three. No being a tightwad, make it snappy."

"I feel like if you put it like that, the spirit of Christmas will just get mad at you…"

The first miracle occurred.

All the bells on the giant fir began to ring. A joyous sound.

And as they did, little Masato's body began to grow.

"Oh! I'm growing!"

"You didn't exactly behave yourself in the toy shop, but the four of you went around together, so you must have registered as good children. How very generous."

"Thanks for keeping the bar so low! Come on! Let's make this the last spurt and be back to normal!"

Masato strained every muscle in his body, willing himself to get bigger.

The child clothes grew very tight, with top, bottom, and underwear all ripping!

Masato was back to normal! He had regained the form of a fifteen-year-old boy! …Albeit nude.

"Augh, noooooo! This is baaaaad!"

"It's a bit…" *Avoid.*

"…hard to look directly at…" *Avoid.*

"I-I-I-I'm not looking!" *Glance.*

While the girls all looked away, Shiraaase approached with a ruler. "Stop that!" "No?" "What a shame." Santa Mamako had whipped out her handbook to record her son's growth, but he forbade that, too.

Whatever. He hastily donned the gear Porta was throwing him, and he was back to normal.

Mm. Wait. If I'm back to normal…are the Kings?

Had they ripped out of their clothes, too?

Amante's sleekly muscled body, bursting out…Sorella's significant assets, spilling free…Fratello's modest behind, shaking…

If he just glanced in their direction, he might well see all of that!

"Tee-hee. Masato." *Grin.*

"No, I'm not thinking anything weird! Please. Trust me!"

Hahako's face had appeared less than an inch from his, and that smile was definitely not a genuine one. It was terrifying. Behind her the Libere crew were hastily getting dressed.

All three were back to normal as well.

"We're all old enough that we don't need a mother anymore! What a relief."

"But we definitely still qualify as kids. At any rate, *our* main problem has been dealt with. Hooray for Christmas miracles. And following on that, can we get—?"

"Oh, Christmas tree! These girls are acting very odd! Could you please cure them?"

"That's what I was about to say, but fine."

The giant Christmas tree answered Santa Mamako's request.

Its glittering limbs rustled, and three human-shaped cookies came floating gently down. One to Wise, one to Medhi, and one to Porta.

"Oh, I know these! Christmas cookies! Um…g-gin something."

"You clearly have no idea. These are gingerbread men. A mildly sweet cookie with plenty of ginger mixed into the dough. Sometimes they're even hung from the tree."

"What a nice smell! I bet these taste good! I can't wait to try them!"

They all took a big bite.

""""Mm!""""

Squeals of delight echoed all around, and they took another bite. And another. As they devoured their cookies…

Their eyes suddenly went wide.

"Mmph! I fink I'm mmpph mmph head is mmpph mmmph at last!"

"I believe mmph mmph we can talk mmph mmph Masato mm-mm-mmph listen mmph!"

"Mo-mmph-ne-mmph is in mmph mmmphhh trouble!"

"How about you talk when your mouths are empty?"

Munch, munch, gulp.

Then the three girls swarmed Masato, beside themselves.

"Listen! After we split up in Thermo, it all went wrong! Mone's in a real bad state! She's seriously messed up!"

"Calm down. How bad are we talking?"

"Her cravings went wild! She'd been trying too hard to go without spoiling, and couldn't hold back anymore! I think something's affecting her mind, too."

"Mone's lost control? Uh-oh."

"And then a hole opened in her chest and we were all sucked in!"

"And next thing we knew, we were in the toy shop and being forced to work! We were under some pretty intense mind control! And why didn't you notice?! You're so stupid, Masato!"

"Don't blame me! I thought something was up, but you kept saying you were fine! I figured out you were brainwashed eventually, so let me off the hook here! Also, where is Mone now?"

"She's right over there," Hahako said, pointing to the top of the giant Christmas tree.

A girl was floating in front of the gold star.

"Whoa, this is amazing! The origin of Christmas! Spreading spoiling across the world! This is what I wanted..."

He knew those clothes. But the gaping hole in her chest was wholly unfamiliar.

It was Mone, with three sets of bat-like wings on her back.

"Um, what the hell is that? Since when does she have wings? And she's flying?! ...Argh, and I'm supposed to be the hero of the heavens! I'm kind of jealous, honestly!"

"Masato, you idiot! This is no time for jokes! Hey, Mone! What are you doing?"

"Dark God Mammone! Stop fluttering around and come down here!"

Mone reacted to that name, glancing their way—but only momentarily.

She reached her arms out toward the gold star. The air in front of her trembled and was sucked into the hole...and the gold star grew distorted. Before long, it also disappeared into the hole.

The bright glow of the giant Christmas tree began to fade.

"Oh no!" Dark-Mom Deathmother wailed, firing up her tablet. "At this rate, Christmas will end! Shiraaase!"

"I am aware. We must stop her."

Shiraaase opened her own device and began tapping on her keyboard. "What...is this?"

"Removal of the decorations signals the end of Christmas!"

"If it ends before you achieve the most important goals, there's no point! For now, Hotta and I will use our admin privileges to delay the end of event processing."

"The programming is far too complicated, so maintaining the status quo is the best we can do! That doesn't solve the real issue. Everyone, hurry! Retrieve the gold star and put it back where it belongs! That's the only way to save Christmas!"

"If Shiraaase's so worried she's stopped calling you Deathmother... r-right, we'll do something ASAP!"

They had to recover the decorations Mone had inhaled. Their goal was clear, but lots of problems lay in their way.

She was their friend. And floating high above them.

"Masato Oosuki! Your attacks will hit! Knock her out of the sky!"

"Don't be ridiculous! That's Mone! I can't hurt her!"

"But why noooot? She's ruining Christmaaaas. She deserves to be mildly blown uuuuup."

"Um, Sorella? How exactly do you *mildly* blow someone up?"

When Masato did nothing, Sorella hopped aboard her giant tome, flying up to Mone.

"Mwa-ha-haaaaaa! Mone isn't the only one who can flyyyyy! I'm gonna get a biiiit rough, but don't worry about thaaaat. *Spara la magia...*"

"I don't mind. In fact, I have no mercy for any kids who don't know how to be spoiled."

"Huh? Gah!"

Mone was suddenly right next to her, burying her fist in Sorella's gut.

The blow was so hard, it knocked Sorella out. She was tossed aside, and she and her tome went into a tailspin, falling toward the ground.

"Sorella?!" Amante tried to run to her, but...

Hahako reached the landing zone first and gently caught her.

"Hahako...well done! I'll thank you on Sorella's behalf."

"Tee-hee. You're welcome. Can you tend to her wounds? I've got something to take care of."

The warm smile she directed toward her children froze over, and Hahako drew her twin Holy Swords.

Santa Mamako tried to stop her, but it was too late. Hahako bounded up the limbs of the giant Christmas tree, hurtling toward her foe.

"Yay! Hahako! Come on! Hahako!"

"Oh my, you certainly seem excited. But what you've done is not so easily forgiven. You must be punished."

Hahako unleashed her full strength. Two attacks struck Mone, one crimson, one navy blue, forming a cross that ravaged her body...or should have.

But when she raised her arms with unbridled fury—someone grabbed them, stopping her.

"Huh...?"

"Tee-hee! Hahako! *Rubrub! Rubrub!* Mwa-haha!"

Hahako's arms were pushed back, her chest exposed—to Mone's cheek rubs. Very clingy. Inseparable.

"I knew it! You've got so much spoiling to give, Hahako! So much mom power! You've gotta have a mom to spoil you! *Rubrub!*"

"H-hey, don't...what's going on...my strength is...draining..."

Hahako sprouted white hands all over, trying to peel Mone off.

But countless black hands emerged from Mone's wings, grabbing and inhaling the white hands.

All strength left Hahako's body. Still entwined with Mone, they fell...and hit the snow together.

"You're kidding... She beat Hahako?!"

"You've gone too far, Dark God Mammone! Hah!"

"Knock it off, ya darn fool! Mahhhhhh!"

Amante and Fratello threw themselves into the snow cloud raised by the impact of their landing.

Sword and fist swung toward the figure within. Both attacks hit home!

The impact of the blow cleared the snow cloud and sent Amante and Fratello flying backward.

And Masato saw...

"Uh, Mone…? What the…?"

The clothes she'd been wearing were gone. She was now decked in the garb of a Dark God, manifested from the power pouring out of her. Shield-like, scalelike, jade-colored armor had brushed aside the girls' attacks like they were nothing.

There was a carefree smile on Mone's lips. And a single horn on her forehead.

"Unspoiled children's attacks won't work on me! This is a breeze!"

"Mone, what is going on with you?"

"She must have inhaled spoil energy from Hahako and converted it into sustenance… A-anyway…Wise!"

"I know! We've gotta make her stop! One solid blow and—"

"Oh? I can sense even stronger spoiling power! Where is it coming from? Over here?"

"Where are you going, Mone?! Come back and face us!"

Maybe she'd lost her memory. She was certainly in full-blown Dark God mode. Dark God Mammone didn't even glance at Wise and Medhi. She started circling the base of the giant Christmas tree.

"Around here somewhere… Oh, here!"

She stopped suddenly, digging into the snow…and pulled out a white bag.

The bag of presents. Dark-Mom Deathmother had buried it there so the children wouldn't find it.

"Wow! Wow! There's so much spoiled energy in here! It's all mine now!"

"Mone, stop! Not that! Those are for…!"

"Wait, don't do that! Those are important…!"

But it was too late.

The hole in Dark God Mammone's chest inhaled the bag…and when they came running, it inhaled Santa Mamako and Hahako, too.

The rest of the party froze. Their brains were unable to process what they had just witnessed.

"Mwa-ha! So good! So good! I need more! More more more!"

Dark God Mammone's body writhed with ecstasy, and she flew up into the air, arms spread wide.

Meanwhile, in a home in the Catharn capital…

Sitting around a table, decked out for Christmas Eve, a mother and a young child traded looks of confusion.

"Mommy, why did it stop snowing?"

"Hmm, good question. Everything is usually covered in snow during Christmas here."

"What happened to the Christmas tree in the other room? Why did it stop glowing?"

"Good question. I thought that was odd…but don't worry. Daddy's looking at the tree. You hurry up and eat! Santa's coming today, so you need to go to bed early."

"Mm! I'm eating!"

The mother patted her son's head as he munched on a meatball. Then she got up and headed to the bedroom she and her husband shared.

"It feels like everything's going wrong…I just have to make sure I can get him his present."

She was checking the present hidden in the closet, just to be sure.

But when she looked in her room, the closet was open—and the window.

A box wrapped in a blue ribbon was floating through the air, out the window.

"Wha—but why?! Stop!"

She ran to it, leaning out the window, desperately stretching her arms out—but it was out of reach.

"Wh-what's going on? What's the meaning of this?"

Then the mother saw Christmas presents floating through the air all over the city, flying down the streets to the north. Away from their homes.

"Mommy, what's wrong?"

"Gasp...n-nothing! Be a good boy and don't look outside. If you're naughty, Santa won't bring you a present!"

"Okay!"

She hid the truth as best she could. It would never do for the children to find out.

This was not the only such mother. Parents the world over were reeling in horror.

Helplessly watching as their precious memories were snatched away.

Back at the peak of Mount Motherest...

Presents had flown in from all directions, and Mone had inhaled them all.

"Hooray! So many! I feel so fulfilled!"

When she swallowed the last of them, Dark God Mammone was inhaled into her own hole...and vanished.

Silence fell. Nothing but silence.

Masato was on his knees. He hadn't planned it. It had just happened.

"Uh...what the...?"

"Masato! No time to collapse! Get a grip!" Dark-Mom Deathmother yelled. She was running her fingers over the tablet screen, sparing only a brief glare in his direction. "Accept the situation! Mone has gone full Dark God! She's craving spoiling and happily stealing it! And she's inhaled both Mamako and Hahako! This is really happening!"

"Y-yeah...I know that, but..."

"So what about it?" Shiraaase said. "Go on, if you kids want to have a Christmas party without the grown-ups, go right ahead. We've got the party venue all set up and ready to go."

This was unusually cold, even for her. She must really be buried in work.

But it helped him gather his wits.

He left a fist print in the snow.

"Oh, we'll have that Christmas party. *With* our moms."

Masato got to his feet.

He turned to his comrades. Wise had been standing, stunned, but she slapped her own cheeks, snapping herself out of it. Medhi had been sitting down, but she forced a smile and got to her feet. Porta quickly started taking recovery items out of her bag, checking her inventory, nodding earnestly.

They're good to go. Next...

The three Kings were still sitting on the cold snow. Amante was a Magic Fencer and had access to basic healing spells, so she was busy tending to Sorella's substantial injuries. Fratello must have suffered some damage during the attack as well. She was clutching her arm, waiting her turn.

Amante shot Masato a look that said, "Don't mind us."

It looked like the four members of Masato's core party were the only people going anywhere fast.

"...Right, listen up, guys. I just wanna say this before anything else."

"Yeah, yeah, you've got no plan. You never do," said Wise.

"And somehow it'll all work out, just like it always does," added Medhi.

"Yes! That's how we do things!" agreed Porta.

"Are we really just improvising our way through every adventure? Yeah, maybe you're right..."

That slapdash approach felt welcome. He felt a weight lift off his shoulders. But he let the smile fade.

"We're gonna go get Mom, Hahako, and all those presents back. But Mone vanished, and we don't know where she is. We have no idea where to even begin. Which means...we're gonna have to depend on others."

"Wow, is that *not* something a hero should say while trying to look like a bad ass."

"I know! Shut up. Anyway, it's worth a shot!"

Masato moved over to the giant Christmas tree and put his hands on the trunk.

Betting on a Christmas miracle.

I may not be the best kid, but please. Tell me how to reach my mom. That's the only Christmas present I need this year.

In the face of his true, heartfelt desire, everything else was forgotten.

And his prayer was answered.

"......Mm? What?"

The giant Christmas tree gently swayed. Several hook-shaped, red-and-white-striped staves descended between the glowing branches toward them.

"These are...I've seen them before, but... Professor Medhi, you know everything. Explain."

"Candy canes! Like gingerbread men, they're often used as edible tree decorations."

"Ohh, candy?"

He picked up a candy cane and gave it a lick. It was sweet. Minty.

"But what do we do with them? Will the sweetness lure Mone back? Doesn't seem like it..."

"Masato! I think I know! We do this!"

Porta took a candy cane, stuck it in the snow, and let go.

The candy cane fell over, pointing to Dark-Mom Deathmother.

"See?"

"O-oh! I get it. Like when you go whichever way a stick points you? Hard to believe this will just show us the way..."

"Then we'll just have to prove it! Porta, can you do that a few more times?"

"Okay! I will!"

Porta lifted the candy cane again and let go. Once again, it fell pointing at Dark-Mom Deathmother. And a third time. Still all Deathmother.

The fourth time she tried leaning it the other way so it wouldn't fall toward Deathmother...but it did a funky spin and somehow ended up pointing at Porta's mom anyway.

"I thought so! The tree gave us these candy canes. They're a sweet item that points toward the wielder's mother."

"Of course those canes are sweet! They're made of candy!"

"Shiraaase, shut up and work. Anyway, this means…"

"It's all you, Masato. Oosuki family bonds, take it away!"

"I don't think this is something only Masato can do, though. The stolen presents included ones Kazuno, Medhimama, and myself prepared. If the canes can detect a mother's feelings, they'll show you girls your way forward, too."

"What, really? My mom actually got me a present? No way! Next thing you know, it'll be snowing in… Oh, I guess it is snowing."

"Well, if that's the case, that's all the more reason to get them back," said Medhi.

"Yes! I really want to get my mommy's Christmas present back!"

Wise was playing up her *tsundere* act, but even she craved her mother's affection.

Everyone lined up and dropped their canes…and they all pointed the same way. Toward a gate shaped like an upside-down J—a gate opened in space itself, leading somewhere else entirely!

It was really narrow.

"What the—! How are we supposed to fit through that?"

"Yeah, even I can't do it…not 'cause I'm flat-chested or anything!"

"Wise, this is no time for friendly fire… Especially on yourself."

"Oooh, what do we do?"

At least get the flat girl through! He tried pushing…

"Ow! My face! My butt!"

But it didn't work. He had a feeling it wouldn't.

But Masato had no other ideas.

"Sheesh, I guess you can't do *anything* without us."

At this display of arrogance, they turned to find the Libere Kings, all healed up and wielding candy canes.

Three more canes fell toward the cane-shaped gate. The gate expanded.

"Oh…"

"Humph. I don't need to explain this, but…"

"We're not trying to save Hahakoooo. But we do want to pay Mone back for what she diiiiid. Get iiiit? I think it's worth explaining this tiiiime."

"Mm. What she said."

"You all know perfectly well these items lead you to your mother, but…fine, we'll go with your version."

There were now seven of them. They were probably, no, definitely the most powerful party in the world, the undefeatable heroes.

"Please, everyone. We have to make this Christmas event a success. For the people of this world…and so the children I personally messed up can find themselves a loving family and lead happy lives. Their fate is in your hands."

Dark-Mom Deathmother made no effort to hide the desperation in her plea.

The Libere Kings seemed to want to respond, but they turned their backs instead. Masato nodded on their behalf.

They then traveled through the candy-cane gate!

But it was still very narrow. "So not cool…" They had to form a single line and then raise both hands over their heads, mimicking the gate's shape, sidling like crabs through it. Like real heroes.

"Masato Oosuki! A moment, please."

"What's up, Amante?"

"I feel like we could have fit through without raising our arms above our heads."

"That is a good point. I realized after going through that it would have been much easier if I'd left my hands at my sides."

At any rate, there was a town on the other side of the gate.

The streets were paved with cookies. The planks in the walls were chocolate. There was a river of soda. Overpoweringly sweet smells wafted in from all directions.

"Whoa! It's a candy town! This is amazing! This is the best thing ever!"

"It is impressive, but…we can't really celebrate like Porta is," said Wise. "We're old enough to be worrying about calories…"

"I'm against obesity and cavities, and sugar won't help your boob size. You're making the right decision," Medhi said, smiling.

"Yeah, yeah, I'm just gonna ignore you."

Masato took a peek inside one of the houses, rude though it was. There were candy people inside.

A mother cuddling with a child, another child getting fed, another on a lap pillow…sweet spoiling everywhere.

"She gathered all the sweeeeetness, and made herself a dream toooown."

"It's sickly sweet. Nothing manly here! Right, sonny?"

"Don't worry, Fratello. The passionate twist we crave is about to arrive."

As they headed down the road, a shrill insectoid whine came from all directions.

Spider fairies. Forming flying battalions, their barbed protrusions thrusting forward.

"Masato, it's those things! They attacked us at the toy store and placed us under their control! Since when do spiders fly?"

"I dunno much about spider biology, but I know these things suck. Don't let them stab you!"

"Recovery magic won't heal you if you get hit. You can balance out the saccharine secretion from the stab with less sweet foods. That'll allow you to recover a bit, but…"

"That's why I brought these from the kitchen the mommies were using!"

Porta reached into her shoulder bag and triumphantly pulled out…green peppers. The enemy of children everywhere. The green bells of spite.

"That's not 'less sweet,' it's straight-up nasty!"

"It's like a punishmeeeeent. If you don't wanna bite into a raaaaaw pepper, then make sure none of these things hit youuuuu."

"Urp...I don't like green peppers, either, so I'll run as fast as I can!"

"You're still a kid, Porta. Not me. I ain't afraid of no peppers."

"Then you can carry them, Fratello! Please! Here!"

Porta happily held them out, clearly loath even to have them on her person.

Fratello's dazed eyes focused momentarily on the peppers, and then she spun on her heel.

"She ran for it." "Totallyyyyy."

Right toward the spider fairies.

Fratello made the first attack, putting her fear-boosted speed behind it.

"Mah!"

Her battle cry was always disproportionately adorable, but her fist struck a squadron of spider fairies and pulverized them. However...

When the needles in their mouths shattered, the air filled with the smell of condensed milk, and a thick white fluid splattered all over Fratello's face.

She turned back to them, eyes glistening, lips quivering.

"Sonny, I'm all sticky." Ooh-lah-lah.

"Y-yeah, I can see that. Just...don't look this way. Someone'll clean you up later."

"You're a mess, Fratello! Attack better!"

"Fiiiine. I'll show you how it's doooone. Mwa-ha-haaaaa."

Fratello was distracted by the goo and had failed to notice more spider fairies approaching. Amante saw this and was on them in a flash, shattering the cookie pavement as she leaped forward.

"You just gotta watch those needles! Like this!"

She unleashed a flurry of stab attacks, piercing one spider fairy after another. "Oh, they're stuck..." One spider fairy after another wound up on her blade.

Her rapier was now a spider kebab.

"Skewed spiders, anyone? I'm not grilling this with *any* kind of marinade."

"You want them griiiilled? Then how about a little fiiiire? ...*Spara la magia per mirare... Fuoco Fiamma!*"

"Er, wait—!"

Sorella's spell activated. The skewered spider fairies were slow roasted over an open flame. The smell of baked goods filled the air.

But the heat made the needles shatter. Splat.

Her face covered in white goo, Amante looked absolutely mortified. Sorella scooped up a finger and tasted it, her bleary eyes filled with bliss. They both turned and walked right toward Masato.

"M-Masato Oosuki! This isn't what it looks like! It's an accident! Just an accident!" Ooh-lah-lah.

"Masatooo! Look! Look! I'm all stiiiicky! Mwa-ha-haaaa!" Ooh-lah-laaaah.

"I get it already; stop trying to make me look! Wipe it off!"

"Honestly, what are they *doing*? Medhi, let's clean this up."

"Yes. We are *pure*, so we'll clean this right up...or I'd like to, but—"

"Whoa! Careful, everyone! There's a *lot* of spider fairies coming! From there and there and everywhere!"

Spider fairies were emerging from the soda river, the chocolate buildings, and all the candy around.

There was now an army of spider fairies in all directions, forming ranks and marching forward.

"Wait, wait, wait! Are we in trouble? How are there so many?!"

"Is the fluid they scattered summoning more? E-either way, we can't handle this many! Let's run for it!"

"Run where?!"

"Obviously...Porta! Give Amante a candy cane!"

"W-wait, Masato Oosuki! Why me?!"

"The more times you do it, the more likely you are to accept it, but I don't need to explain *that*!"

"You just did...argh! This is an emergency. Fine, I'll do it!"

The canes pointed them toward their mothers, so they ran in the direction they led them.

The spider fairies didn't fly all that fast. It seemed like they'd be able to push through.

"Good! If we just keep going…!"

"Yep! Right, while I've got a moment…" *Rubrub.*

"Sonny, lemme borrow your jacket sleeve." *Rubrub.*

"Hey, you two! What are you doing? Don't wipe your goo on my gear!"

"Well, it's your faaaault. You've gotta help with the cleanuuuup." *Rubrub.*

"How is it my fault?! Stop talking, Sorella!"

Faces wiped, they ran on. Down winding roads, across intersections, checking their paths with the candy canes. They were making steady progress.

They reached a square with a fountain. At the back was a big door with a kanji character on it. The character could be read as *amai*, which meant both "sweet" and "spoiled."

"Oh! That sure screams 'boss room.' Are we finally gonna face Mone?"

"Yep! I'm not worried about Hahako at all! We're gonna burst right on through! You on board, Masato Oosuki?"

"Sure, sure…actually, no, wait, give me minute."

Masato jogged over to the mountain. He was hoping to quickly wash the sticky white goo off his jacket, but…

"Wait, this fountain is…"

It certainly looked like water flowing through it, but the flow was too viscous.

It moved more like molasses. When he reached out and touched it, it was every bit as sticky.

"Is this some sort of syrup? Yikes, what now?!"

Some of the fountain's liquid had suddenly coalesced, taking shape like a sugar sculpture.

It formed hands, and a head, then started getting more detailed, adding gear and individual hairs.

It was clear at first, but soon color started filling in, revealing…

"Wait, is this *me*?!"

"Yes. I am you, and you are me!"

Another Masato, indistinguishable from the real thing! The copy drew his sword and swung! "Ack!" Masato quickly drew his own, blocking just in the nick of time.

The two Masatos' hilts clashed. This sudden twist left his party reeling...

"I guess we can just beat 'em both up." *Grin.*

"The survivor will be the real one." *Smirk.*

"Don't! The fake is *always* stronger in scenes like this!"

Wise and Medhi easily rattled off strategies that didn't show the least bit of concern for their friend.

Either way, their confidence didn't last long. Six other sections of the fountain burbled upward, each mimicking another person.

Wise, Medhi, Porta, Amante, Sorella, and Fratello. Six more figures between them and the spoiled boss room.

Masato pushed Masato back then leaped back from him, and the other six joined him.

"So you're not letting us in that easy, huh?"

"How obnoxious. Let's clear this obstruction, pronto. I'd like to start by learning the nature of our foe... Porta, can you tell us anything?"

"I'll check it out! ...Hngggg... Those are candy golems! But they aren't bad monsters!"

"Yes! We aren't monsters! We're copies of whoever came here! We exist to judge if those people are worthy of passing through this door!"

"Oh, the other Porta's just as helpful! You're such a good girl that even your copy is nice! I'm so proud."

"We're going to start judging now! Good luck!"

"But there's clearly no time for joking around."

"Exactly! Come at me, me!"

Candy Masato raised Firmamento high and swung it down. The real Masato responded with a side swipe. The vertical and horizontal blows clashed with an earsplitting clang, and both blows were deflected.

"The fight's begun! I don't need to explain this, but we don't wanna attack our own side!"

"This goes without saying, but everyone, make sure you only attack your double!"

"Mm."

"I knew that without y'all saying anything."

Sparks flew everywhere. At the center of the battlefield, Masato, Amante, and Fratello—the three close-range fighters—charged in. Their copies did, too.

Swords and fists clashed, their strength an even match. The only way to shift the balance…

"The real me is gonna offer real support! …*Spara la magia per mirare… Salire!*"

"*My support is better than hers! …Spara la magia per mirare… Salire!*"

Attack buffs took effect simultaneously, blanketing both combat teams.

And both backline support Clerics glared at each other. "Heh-heh-heh, what does that even mean?" "*It's a simple statement of fact.*" They both flashed their prettiest smiles and stepped onto the front line, dark power gushing out, staves raised high—and blows rained down.

"Yo, Medhi! Why is our healer on the front line? This is exactly the kind of situation we need to maintain our core strategy! Geez!"

"Blunt instrumeeeents are so scaaaary. You're a Maaaage! But so prone to violeeeence!"

"*I knoooow! What kind of Mage gets physicaaaaal? At times like thiiiis…*"

"*You want to go all in on the magic! Use the biggest spells you can!*"

"You're on! You'd better be ready for me, me!"

The magic attackers summoned magic tomes in their hands or overhead, chanting spells.

"If you're gonna copy me, trying filling out a bit! Show me what I've always dreamed of being! …*Spara la magia per mirare… Forte Fiamma Cannone!*"

"*Well, I can't have what you don't! I'm the one wants to cry about it!* …Spara la magia per mirare… Forte Ghiaccio Cannone!"

Wise vs Candy Wise. Both glaring at one body part—I won't say what.

Two types of cannonfire—one, extremely concentrated flames, the other, ice cold enough to freeze the soul—were unleashed at the same time. When they met, the sound was so loud, it was like space-time rupturing, shaking everything in the vicinity.

Especially the things the Sorellas had (and the Wises didn't).

The Sorellas glared at each other.

"My, myyyy. Aren't the children livelyyyy."

"Lively isn't baaad, but flashy spells aren't betterrrr."

"I knoooow! It's so much classier to just drain the life from someooooone. *Spara la magia per mirare… Veleno Sospiro!*"

"What's really elegant are damage-over-time (DoT) spells. That's what the real ladies favooor. *Spara la magia per mirare… Maledizione Nebbia!*"

A poisonous wind, and a cursed one. Winds blew across the battle-field from both directions, meeting in the center.

One touch spelled doom. It entered through the skin, rampaging through the body. Certain, unavoidable death… "Hey!" *"Are you try-ing to kill your own side?!"* ""Whaaaat?"" Both the real and the copy Sorella turned and fled.

"This calls for the hero chosen by the heavens!"

"One attack from me will slice this air asunder!"

The two shock waves scattered the malevolent winds, and the Holy Swords clashed once again. How many times now? All parties resumed their attacks.

"Whoa…this is way more spectacular than usual!"

"Me! That place isn't safe! Come over here!"

"O-okay! I'll go stand with me!"

Porta and Candy Porta hid together, hand in hand, closely watching the fierce battle between originals and copies.

But there was a clear difference between the two sides.

How long had the fight been going on?

"Come on, me! Keep them feet moving!"

"Sh-shut up! Hah...hah...they're moving, see?"

They were evenly matched. But as time went on, the gap between those who knew fatigue and those who never grew tired became clear.

Copy Masato was still waving that sword around like it weighed nothing. But the real one had built up so much lactic acid, he could barely lift his arms. "Crap!" Unable to lift his blade in time to block or raise his arm to deploy his shield wall, he was forced to evade the attack by rolling across the ground.

Damn, I'm in trouble. He's really got me on the ropes!

His party was not faring any better.

The magic cannon team had run out of magic. "It's all yours!" "I caaaan't?!" And too tired to run around. Wise and Sorella were using the magic tome as a shield, weathering a storm of fire and ice.

Medhi had thrown herself into the front line but retreated the moment she found herself at a disadvantage. She'd clearly planned (diabolically) to elegantly spectate, but...

"Clever trick, if I do say so myself."

"Gah...!"

Candy Medhi fired off a bind spell that left her unable to move.

Amante had been displaying superhuman physical abilities, but even she was on her knees.

"Ha! Serves you right."

"Time to concede!"

"Tch!"

Fratello had collapsed, so Amante had been carrying her and fighting off both their copies, but it looked like she couldn't hold out any longer.

Was this the moment of their doom?

"Hey, me! You can't be looking all over the place! Focus!"

"Yikes! Time out! Please, gimme a moment! Yeah, no way you're gonna listen..."

"Okay, sure."

Copy Masato stopped mid-swing.

All the other copies stopped, too.

"Um, what's this about? You're just gonna comply? That's awfully sweet of you."

"Of course! We're made of candy! We're basically complete suckers."

"I can't believe you just casually said that with my face and voice…"

"It's the truth! We're such suckers, we'll take pity on our enemy mid-battle! It makes perfect sense. I mean, I'm a sweetheart. A sucker. A naive, spoiled Momma's boy. What could be better?"

"Oh God, shut up! They might think those are *my* true feelings! Listen, everyone, none of that's true! That's not me talking!"

"Wait, Masato! That is Masato!"

"Yes! I know it! That's Masato!"

When Masato tried to deny it, Porta and Candy Porta came running.

"Wow, cuteness twofold. No, wait, putting that statement in surround sound doesn't make it true!"

"S-sorry! But it's important to accept the sweetness of spoiling! If you can't do that, you won't get past this door! I taught myself this!"

"Er…what does that mean?"

"We judge if people have accepted the sweetness of spoiling! Like this!"

Candy Porta turned to Porta.

"Me! I love my mommy! So I want her to spoil me a lot! What do you think, me?"

"I also love my mommy! I love being spoiled! I'm just like you, me!"

"Yes! You're okay! You've been cleared!"

We're the same! The same! They smiled, clasped hands, and Copy Porta faded out.

The kanji for *spoiled* began flashing in the air above Porta's head. She was clear to proceed!

"You see, Masato?!"

"I've got to accept the spoiled stuff I'm saying? Seriously? The dungeon of spoiling is way too tough…this is more like…someone's hardcore shame fetish."

"But it's our only option, right? We gotta do it."

"Yes. If you think about it, it may be the perfect opportunity."

Wise and Medhi nodded and approached their own copies.

Wise first.

"I know you know this, but I loathe my mom."

"You say that, but you can't really bring yourself to hate her. She's your mom, after all. And that's just the way she is. She acts like a proper mom every now and then, and that's all it takes for you to forgive her."

"Yeah. I'm the one spoiling her. You say you're a sucker, but so am I. I admit it, so go on, vanish already. You're embarrassing."

They both huffed angrily then high-fived as they walked past each other. Copy Wise vanished.

Medhi next.

"I have always let Mother spoil me."

"I know. We believed that was the right thing to do, never tried to think for ourselves, and just let her make all our decisions. And bottled up all our frustrations until they exploded."

"But my mother accepted that selfishness. I should be working to make that up to her, but instead I'm off enjoying an adventure. If that isn't spoiled, I don't know what is."

"We're basking in the sweetness of our mother's love."

"Precisely."

Their identical eyes winced, and they held out their hands…

Thnk! Two staves, each swinging for the other's shin, clashed. The dark-powered girls smirked, and the candy copy vanished.

Wise and Medhi had accepted their own spoiled sides.

"Right."

"You're up, Masato."

"…Yeah, fine."

Honestly, he really didn't want to, but…

The perfect opportunity, huh? Maybe she's right.

Medhi's words had struck a nerve. And that got him to his feet.

Without drawing attention to it, he checked that the Libere Kings were watching and turned to face his copy.

"First, I don't even want to *consider* letting Mom or any other mom spoil me."

"Wait, Masato? What are you saying?"

"I know how you feel, but this isn't the time…!"

"Calm down! I know! But I gotta be honest, right? You're me, so you know, right?"

What was Masato trying to say? What would saying it accomplish? Of course it knew. Copy Masato nodded.

"I can't stop myself from pushing her back. That's just how it is. Typical teenager stuff."

"Exactly. I'm in the proverbial 'rebellious phase.' I argue with my parents, act like a know-it-all, look down on them, sometimes I get so mad, I even raise a fist and make threats…but this is something that happens to everyone. To every child. It's as if that's how we were programmed to act."

The three Kings were watching intently. Masato was acutely aware of their stares and spoke as clearly as he could.

"I want to do better, but I can't. It just doesn't work that way. I've got to accept that. And that sucks, but…most families manage to get through it. I dunno how."

"Because they're suckers. Spoiled. And sweet."

"Yeah, maybe. I've said all kinds of awful shit to her, lashed out like crazy. Looking back on it, maybe I always knew deep down that she'd forgive me for it."

"That's pretty spoiled. But our mom handled all of that."

"She accepted that this is how all teenagers are, and that's okay. In the end, she always gave me a hug. I've been letting her spoil me the whole time. It was spoiling that brought me here. I can protest that I don't *want* it all I like, but it doesn't mean anything. What will mean something is accepting the truth. However reluctantly."

"Reluctant it may be, but that's the best we can do."

"Yeah. That's me."

They fist-bumped, nodded, and Candy Masato vanished.

And along with him went the last shred of Masato's need to rebel against Mamako.

Putting it all out there does feel good. It's like a weight off my shoulders.
Then he remembered.

MMMMMORPG (working title) stood for Mom's Massively Maternal Multiplayer Making-up-with-Offspring Role-Playing Game.

It was a game where parents and children with relationship issues formed a party and went on adventures with the goal of getting closer together.

Masato had entered this world as a hero and had now found himself. He'd broken down the walls he'd built up and taken a step closer to his mother.

Perhaps he'd found one of the answers that lay at the end of this family journey. He felt like he had anyway.

"I just meant to help these three along, but...maybe I was the one who needed that last push. Either way..."

Everyone rebels against their parents. There was nothing children could do to stop themselves from doing it.

And if your mother could accept that and wait for you with arms open wide, all you had to do was throw yourself into them.

Had the three girls understood that? He turned to look.

"...Humph. How idiotic." Amante snarled.

She turned to face her copy.

They both folded their arms, lording it over the other. They glowered at each other wordlessly.

"If you're us, then you oughtta know. Work it out."

"Yes. Do as you please."

Copy Amante, Copy Sorella, and Copy Fratello all smiled faintly, and vanished.

Everyone present had been cleared. The door bearing the kanji for *amai* opened. Amante led the way with the other two Four Kings following right behind.

"Um, wait up! You all accepted your spoiling? How?"

"Not telliiiing. It's a seeecret. Mwa-ha-haaaa."

"Men don't use words. They talk with their backs."

"Yep. This is our personal problem. No need to explain it to you. Humph."

"This would be a good time to accidentally explain it…"

They seemed extra grumpy. Masato shook his head, and his party followed them in.

The Dark God lay at the source of that sweet-smelling breeze.

A Christmas Memory

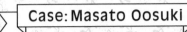

Porta

I want to hear your memory, Masato!

Uh, lemme see. I mostly remember bad things...

Masato

Wise

Bad things? Like what?

Like, right before Christmas, everyone would get all chummy with me and want me to throw a party at my place. It was rough turning them all down.

Masato

Medhi

I get it. They were after Mamako's cooking...or Mamako herself.

Aw, Ma-kun, you wanted the party to be just the two of us? Tee-hee!

Mamako

Masato

That is *not* what I said!

MERRY CHRISTMAS, MASATO OOSUKI

Chapter 5 I Don't Want to Call This the Miracle of the Holy Night. This Is the Result of One Family's Hard Work.

Behind the door it was nothing like the classy candy town. This space was covered in magical patterns.

A zone hidden from the world. The Dark God's domain.

It was immense. A deep pit with no visible bottom, only a magic circle serving as a floor over the depths.

All around them were magic circles laden with stolen presents. Boxes and bundles, lovingly wrapped. Somewhere in there was the white bag with the presents from their mothers.

It seemed like she was extracting the essence of spoiling from these piles. The magic circles supporting the presents were dropping marshmallow-like objects, and someone was eating them as fast as they arrived.

The Dark God, Mammone.

"Oh, there you are! Hey, hey! Welcome! Make yourselves at home!"

Dark God Mammone waved at them with both hands. She lay sprawled out at the center of the main magic circle, her head resting on the laps of a very confused Santa Mamako and Hahako.

A single horn on her head, six wings on her back, power flowing out of her body and manifesting as armor—Mone was every bit the Dark God. Absorbing this sight, the party stood at the edge of the magic circle floor.

"She seems glad to see us... So what now?"

"Well, at least words work, but I don't think chatting is gonna help here. Back at the tree, she beat the snot out of the Kings..."

"She did not! We let her off easy." Amante raised her rapier. "Dark God Mammone! I've got a lot I want to say to you—but first, revenge!"

"Hey, doesn't talking usually come first?!"

Masato reached out a hand to stop her, but Amante nimbly slipped past it, using her explosive speed to cross the circle over to Mammone. "Hahh!" A merciless stab, the sharp tip—

…easily caught between two of Dark God Mammone's fingers.

Snap. Like breaking a pretzel.

"Wh…that easily?!"

"Please. You're so slow! Try to take this seriously."

"Then I'll just have to overpower ya! Mah!"

Fratello had used Amante to hide her approach, popping out and unleashing her ultimate move—a punch, wrapped in a combat aura, with a high crit rate—

One wing flapped, kicking up a powerful wind that easily pushed Fratello's fist back. And her entire body. "Mah?!" "Hey?!" And Amante, too—both went flying.

"Crap! We're gonna fall through—Sorella!"

"I knooooow! Super-uuuurgent!"

As the two went flying over the party's heads, Sorella hopped on her magic tome, flying after them.

She managed to catch them just before they plunged into the abyss. Barely.

"She did it! Whew! I'll go heal them!" said Porta.

"Don't hold off on the buff items, either! No being stingy here!" shouted Masato.

Porta raced off to the Libere Kings. Masato watched her go then drew his sword.

Wise had her magic tome out. Medhi swung her staff a few times. They were ready.

Dark God Mammone had her head on the mothers' laps, rubbing her cheeks against them in a very spoiled fashion. She gave the party an irritated look and slowly got to her feet.

"Ew, what now? You're looking for a fight? Why?"

"That's up to you. If you give us Mom and Hahako back and then return all the presents you stole, I'll let you off with a single punch."

"Huh? Give them back? Pfff, what are you even talking about? Everything here is *mine*. The presents, and these mommies. Right, Mamako-mama? Hahako-mama?"

Santa Mamako and Hahako both slowly nodded.

Looking deeply concerned.

"They've been brainwashed, just like we were."

"Not fully, though. Still...to control those two, both at the same time—she certainly has the power of a secret boss from a top-tier quest."

"Thank you, thank you. Yes, I'm very strong! But let me correct one thing. I'm not brainwashing anyone! I'm connected to these mommies by the power of spoiling."

"At least say 'the power of love.'"

"Oh, are you jealous? If you ask nicely, I could let you borrow one for a moment."

"Are you serious? *We're* the ones letting you borrow *them*!"

Masato started running toward Dark God Mammone. Not that fast, though.

He was trying to formulate a plan of attack.

First, I've gotta free Mom and Hahako...and to do that...

As he reached Dark God Mammone, he swung his blade sideways.

Trying to startle her. Make her flinch and move away from the moms.

"Mm? What?"

But Mammone didn't move. She just let the blade hit her. "Augh?!" Masato tried to stop the swing, but it was too late. The Holy Sword Firmamento's honed blade struck the Dark God's neck...

Clang! It bounced off.

She had no barrier. The skin of her neck was simply impenetrable.

"The heck? How much defense do you *have*?!"

"Sorry! I'm just that strong. Oh, I know, that's the Holy Sword of the Heavens, right? How about I do this?"

Dark God Mammone spread her wings, lifting herself into the air. Leaving the mothers unguarded at the center and leaving herself fully exposed to attack. She even beckoned.

"You're getting pretty full of yourself, but fine. I'll go all out. Don't hate me later!"

He focused his mind, raised his spirits and his blade, and swung down! A heroic blow! He unleashed a max-sized, serious-business shock wave!

Dark God Mammone turned her back and stuck her butt out. The shock wave bounced off it, ricocheting to one side.

"Oh no, you split my butt in two!"

"Whaaaaat?! A joke like that, heeeere?! Arghh!" Masato raged, but...

He was pretty calm inside. This situation was what he'd wanted.

Wise! Medhi! Now!

Masato sent out a volley of shock waves, masking the girls' actions.

Dark God Mammone was busy deflecting the shock waves with her rear, so her eyes were turned away from them. This was their opening. They just had to get to Mamako and Hahako, and secretly...

"Aww, you perv...but obviously, I see what you're doing. *Rompi la testa!*"

"Crap! Stop, you two!"

""Huh?!""

Dark God Mammone's spell activated instantly, ignoring the whole spell chant. A massive blade appeared above Wise and Medhi, stretching as far as the eye could see.

The blade fell. The girls froze in their tracks, unable to dodge, staring upward in horror...

But just before it split their heads and bodies in two, Amante swept in at blinding speed, sending the two of them rolling across the magic circle. A narrow escape.

"Oww...I mean, that saved us, but could you be a bit gentler?"

"Ugh...if that leaves scars, you're paying my medical bills."

"Just say thank you, geez!"

Leaving Wise and Medhi where they lay, Amante ran over to Masato.

"Masato Oosuki! Got a sec? I have an idea."

"Interesting, I had one as well. Seemed like she's really against anyone getting closer to our moms."

"Which suggests her unnatural strength is somehow related to them."

"Yes! I thought that, too! Whoa!" Porta yelped. She was riding on the giant magic tome, and clearly nervous about it. Sorella and Fratello were each keeping a hand on her for safety. "I appraised her! The magic circle below us has an effect that absorbs spoil energy and sends it directly to Mone! The effect is stronger the closer you get to the center!"

"Thanks, Porta! That means…"

"Whaaaat?"

"Sonny, what's the plan?"

"…Good question."

He wanted to move Mamako and Hahako away from the center. But Dark God Mammone would be using her full incredible strength to stop that. It kinda felt like they were at an impasse.

Then Amante slapped him hard on the back.

"Just go do something, even if it doesn't work! That's how you always do things. Use the power of spoiling or parent-child bonds or whatever. Just get your mom back."

That got him moving.

"…Can I ask a favor?"

"What?"

"I'll demonstrate first. But you gotta follow my lead. I'll need you to get your mom back. Promise me that."

"Okay, okay, fine, just go…no, wait, whose mom?! You can't just decide that for us!"

"You already agreed! I'm holding you to it!"

Amante made a grab for him, but he dodged. Then he sheathed his sword and took a step toward Mamako.

"Gah! You busybody hero!"

"High firepower, massive busybody. Like mother like son," said Wise. "Guess we'd better back Masato up, huh?"

"Will you three help? Deal with Mone, that is," asked Medhi.

"Humph! I suppose! It needs to be done, after all."

"Right, riiiight. Leave it to uuuus."

"Mm. Gotta help sonny out."

"I'll make some extra-special items and help that way!"

Porta huffed enthusiastically, and everyone smiled at her.

Their support could make or break this battle.

"Ohhh? Don't you go sneaking up to my moms! Not one step closer!"

"Mone! We're your opponents! ...*Spara la magia per mirare... Alto Bomba Sfera!* And! *Alto Bomba Sfera!*"

"Followed byyy... *Spara la magia per mirare... Alto Tornadoooo!*"

"Ugh, magic doesn't work on *me*!"

Wise's twin energy balls exploded, scoring a direct hit on Mammone—but as she said, they did no damage at all.

But they were followed by a tornado. The Dark God was enveloped by explosive winds, completely obscured from view. She couldn't see out of that thing at all.

"Right! Flawless!"

"Now she can't see Masatoooo. It should buy some tiiime..."

"It didn't! Hi!"

Dark God Mammone poked her head out of the tornado with all the ease of someone stepping through a bead curtain. Disaster-force winds not even scratching her. Ridiculously OP.

Medhi had just finished casting *Alto Barriera*, buffing Amante and Fratello's defense. Looking tense, they prepared for combat.

To one side...

"Will it be good? It'll be good! A good item...done! Everyone, grit your teeth!"

Porta had a mask on and had successfully performed Item Creation with the green peppers and a mystery fluid. The result was "Green Pepper Perfume."

The concentrated essence of capsicum was swept up by the winds of the tornado.

"Wait, what's that weird scent... It's b-biiiiiittter?! It's corrupting my sweet spoiling! I hate green peppeeeers! Aiiieeee!"

"Porta's item was super-effective..."

"We don't even have to do nothin'…"

"I did it!" *Heh!*

Her nostrils and tastebuds assaulted, Dark God Mammone was writhing in agony inside the tornado.

They'd successfully bought some time. Time enough to…

Masato reached the center of the magic circle.

"Thanks to my reliable comrades."

Hahako seemed pretty calm. She was kneeling in the center of the spoil-sucking circle, eyes closed, like she was enduring something… but Masato wasn't in any state to worry about that.

Because someone was staggering toward him, a Holy Sword in each hand.

Masato did not draw his.

"Yeah, I saw this coming. She's being mind-controlled, after all."

"S-sorry! I'm trying to fight it, but…!"

Moving stiffly, Santa Mamako tightened her grip on her swords, raising them aloft.

His mom was attacking him.

An icy grip clutched his heart, the worst feeling in the world…

And both swords swung toward him. The power of Mother Earth and Ocean activated!

"Argh…mm? Huh?"

A number of rock spikes popped up. Several water bullets splattered.

They were definitely aimed at Masato, but he just went, "Hup," and easily sidestepped them.

"What the… Did she drain so much spoiling from you, it's made you weak? …No, this is *my* mom. Even brainwashed, I bet she's just spoiling her son. Geez."

Santa Mamako raised her swords again, but Masato closed the gap and grabbed her arms, stopping her.

He could say it now.

"Mom, ever since we started this game…and for a while before that, really…I've been grumbling about you. A lot. I've been a real unpleasant kid."

He closed his eyes, remembering.

She would call his name, and he would barely respond. He would be cranky with her, lash out. He would even threaten to sever their familial ties. He'd done so much wrong.

They weren't pleasant memories for any son.

"Honestly, part of me just couldn't handle you. Especially how close you wanted to be and how you were all over me. And then there's the way you look so young that it's hard to believe you gave birth to me. It's not a nice way to put it, but sometimes I even wondered if you were actually human."

"Ma-kun…"

Speaking the truth was making her eyes wet with tears.

But before they could fall…

"But now that we're adventuring together, I've been forced to rethink many things—because you were here with me. And I finally realized…it's not your fault. I'm the one in the wrong. I couldn't deal with my own emotions, got all frustrated, and then took them out on you. And I did so because I knew you'd spoil me and forgive whatever I did."

Masato bumped his forehead against Mamako's.

"Sorry for all the hardship I've caused you. And thank you."

As he expressed his gratitude, he rubbed his head against hers.

"You're my mom. And I'm your son. If you're gonna spoil anyone, it oughta be me. Come here!"

He put his arms around her.

Everything he'd felt since entering this game, journeying together, poured into a single moment.

Softly stepping past his embarassment.

…*Yep, that's my mom.*

Holding her tightly against him.

He'd released his grip on her hands, fully aware she might attack. He closed his eyes, trusting her, feeling her.

Feeling his mother's warmth in his arms...or...

"Mm? That's more than warm, that's...hot?! And bright?!"

Feeling a sizzling heat, Masato opened his eyes and still couldn't see.

"Wait, is this A Mother's Light? Uh...Mom?!"

"Yes. Mommy is Ma-kun's mommy. And Ma-kun is Mommy's son."

Flash!

This luminosity was getting seriously intense, but she dropped her swords, wrapped her arms around his back, and held him tight.

Sheer joy had evolved her mom skill into **A True Mother's Light**, and the effects of it freed her from Dark God Mammone's control!

"You're back to normal? Victory for family ties! ...Okay, Mom, let go of me! That's enough!"

"No, I want to stay like this longer. Ma-kun, after everything you said...Mommy's just so happy, I'm ready to burst. *Sniff.*" *Fshh.*

"Joy has you so overheated, it's instantly vaporizing your tears! Calm down, please! Argh! Fine, we'll do it like this!"

Scalded by love so hot, it had passed the boiling point, Masato started moving, Santa Mamako clinging tightly to him. Basically dragging her away from the center of the magic circle.

"Bitterrrrrr...er, huh? Yikes!"

Beset by the cloud of green pepper fumes, Dark God Mammone suddenly lost her balance, snatched up by the swirling winds. "That stings!" She was even taking minor damage!

"Mone's weakening! That means...!"

"Masato pulled it off. Well done."

"Masato is amazing! Our trusted hero!"

Seeing Masato dragging a body of light (Santa Mamako) toward them, the girls all put a hand to their eyes—not wiping tears, just shielding them from the light.

And the Kings...

"…Masato Oosuki did it."

"Yeahhh…he showed us the waaay."

"I done made up my mind. Take it away, Amante! It's all yours!"

"I'd rather you *not* just dump this all on me! Humph!"

Sorella and Fratello started poking her, which just made Amante even angrier.

But they didn't have time to goof around. Dark God Mammone came flying out of the tornado.

"Argh! What is this? My strength is…ohhhhh?! Mamako-mama?! Why are you over there? That's not right! Let's get you back where you belong!"

"Not happening! Fratello, let's go!"

"Mm."

When Mammone started rocketing toward Mamako, Amante grabbed Fratello and threw her like a human projectile.

With her tiny fist fully charged, and the full force of the throw behind it, she readied a super-ultimate punch!

"Mahhhhhh!"

"Oh, that shout is so cute! I mean, wait—!"

Dark God Mammone hastily threw up a jade-colored shield, and Fratello's fist struck it!

And the missile punch was strong enough to shatter the shield! "Yikes!" With her shield crumbling, Mammone was sent flying!

Fratello was knocked backward on the rebound, but Sorella's magic tome swooped in and caught her.

"Niiiiice! Another criiiit, you're on a roll todaaaay."

"Mm. Porta's buff item's workin' out real good. Ain't nothin' beatin' me now."

Confidence blazing in her eyes, Fratello raised her fists again, ready for more.

Recovering from the blow in midair, Mammone used her wings to stabilize herself. She might not have been defeated yet, but that blow had definitely done damage.

The spoiled, confident look was gone, and she looked very cross.

"Argh, you're so annoying! Fine, I'll just—"

"She's gonna use a big move! Ha! So obvious. Sage Wise! Cleric Medhi! Defense magic…!"

"I'm just gonna have to get spoiled more!"

"Er, what did she say?"

"Spoils!"

Dark God Mammone's wings flapped once. And she dove directly to the center of the magic circle.

There, she threw her arms around Hahako—who turned quite pale.

"Hahako-mama! These kids are being mean to me! It's so unfair! I need you to spoil me more! So much more! Power!"

"Y-yes. I guess I'll give you…more…"

Hahako didn't look good. The more Dark God Mammone rubbed against her chest and lap, drinking up the spoiling, the more painful the look on Hahako's face became…

A moment later, her outline blurred, like when electromagnetic interference blocks the TV signal.

Masato joined the girls, staring in horror.

"What the…? Mom, you've gotta let go of me! Get your head in the game!"

"Y-you're right. That was very bad. Hahako is about to break."

"Mamako?! Break—how?!" shouted Wise.

"Literally!"

Santa Mamako pulled Masato tight, looking very sad.

"When Mone comes to get spoiled, our strength drains very quickly. We're not strong enough to resist. But that's not the hard part—what hurts is our feelings. As mothers."

"A mother's feelings? How so?" asked Medhi.

"With our real children watching, we have to call another child ours, and dote on them. And because of that, our real children suffer. You wonder what you're even doing, and you get so sad, and upset, and…then…"

"Your heart breaks… That's really bad. Especially for Hahako!" said Masato.

Hahako had a lot of love for the three Kings. It was still one-sided, but it was worth calling genuine maternal affection.

Those feelings were the core of what made Hahako herself.

And if she broke, Hahako would cease to exist.

"Oh no! This is terrible! We have to do something, Masato!" yelled Porta.

"Of course! Come on, everyone! We've gotta peel Mone away from Hahako! That comes first!"

At his cry, Santa Mamako, Wise, Medhi, and Porta nodded.

Sorella and Fratello, too. One opened her giant magic tome, the other charged her fist, and they got ready to attack Dark God Mammone.

But Amante didn't budge.

"Yo, Amante, what are you doing?"

"…What *am* I doing?"

"Huh? This isn't the time! Get ready to fight! Even if your sword's broken, you can help somehow! C'mon!"

But yelling at her didn't seem to work. She was staring at her feet, not moving a muscle.

"Masatooo! Just leave Amante beeee!"

"Mm. No time to dillydally. I'm goin' in! Back me up!"

"Tch, fine! This is your show; we'll support you!"

He glared at Amante one more time, waiting as long as he could, but it was no use. Masato ran off.

Seeing Fratello approaching, Mammone rolled her eyes.

"Argh, what a pain… Fine, I'll just have to swat you."

A guillotine appeared. "Nope!" Masato hit it with a shock wave, trying to delay the fall long enough for Fratello to get by, but even more blades materialized, slicing downward. It was impossible to move forward.

Mammone's attacks kept coming. Her wings opened wide. Gusts of wind, aimed directly at Porta as she tried to get more pepper perfume ready. "Whoa?!" "Oh dear! Porta's flying away!" Santa Mamako grabbed her, and Wise and Medhi threw up barrier spells, weathering the storm.

They were on the defensive, but Sorella had snuck around from the

other direction. She reached out to snatch Hahako, but, "Gotcha!"
"Yiiikes!" Failure. One wing smacked her away.

Amante was just watching.

"...What am I doing?"

Watching her friends fight. Staring at the blade Mammone had broken.

Her feet wouldn't budge.

"Sorella...Fratello...you're so desperate. If Hahako was gone, would that really be so bad? We can live without a mother. There's no real *need* for one."

She asked, but they couldn't hear.

"...Aren't you scared?"

Her whisper was too soft for anyone to hear.

"After all we've done, do you really think anyone would just accept us? Just forgive us? Hahako doesn't know us. There's nothing there. It's not like Masato Oosuki and his mom. There isn't anything tangible connecting us to her."

Amante's head was all the way down now. Then...

Hahako's entire body blurred.

Amante heard the girls scream and looked up—and saw a small booklet floating by Hahako's chest.

"That's... She said the casino manager gave it to her."

The maternal and child health handbook. It was glowing bright, sending waves out around it.

Something similar had happened during the Matriarchal Arts Tournament, but...this was so much weaker, it was downright sad.

Like the final fleeting embers of Hahako's life, holograms of the memories she'd made that day appeared around them.

Hahako gingerly cradling three babies.

Hahako walking along the beach, holding hands with three children.

Hahako looking thoroughly flummoxed by their wails when they realized they'd been tricked into getting their shots at the pediatrician's.

Hahako wrapping the first presents she would ever give them, looking so happy, she seemed ready to weep with joy.

Family memories. Bonds they'd built up.

And the children in those images…

"There *is* a tangible link connecting us to Hahako!"

Amante threw aside her broken sword, slapped her cheeks with both hands, and broke into a run.

She headed toward Hahako as her eyes drank in the memories, the light fading from them. Her pace grew even faster.

"Hey! Clear a path for me! I'm coming in!"

"Amante! Geez, took you long enough!"

"Argh, what a pain… I'm just gonna mow you all down."

Frustrated, Dark God Mammone finally moved away from Hahako. A violent aura of spoiling swirled around her, and a massive scythe appeared in her hands. She swung it at Masato's party.

"She's all buffed up again! If she hits us, it'll be bad news! We've gotta stop her!"

"Ma-kun. Mommy has an idea. What if we get the presents from us mommies back first? Can you do that?"

"I don't get it, but okay! I'm gonna trust you on this one."

He looked around at the present-laden magic circles, spotted the white bag on one, and sent a shock wave flying toward it. "Please!" The shock wave turned into a hawk, collecting the target and bringing it back to them.

Santa Mamako caught the bag and removed a present with a green bow from it. She held it aloft.

"From Mommy Santa to Mone! May my precious feelings reach you!"

This present came from Leene, the woman who'd become Dark God Mammone's mother.

The feelings laden within became a soft glow and a voice: *"Mone, your mother believes in you. You're my daughter, not an evil god."*

"Mommy?! Y-yeah, I'm not an evil god! I'm a good god!"

Dark God Mammone had been about to rampage, but she stopped on a dime, pretending she hadn't.

An opening!

"Noooow!"

"Mm. Hurry!"

Sorella and Fratello swooped in on the giant magic tome, throwing their arms around Hahako.

Dark God Mammone saw them and turned to drive them off, but...

"Don't you dare! Hah!" Porta sprang to her feet and started waving a fan she'd sprinkled with pepper perfume. "Ughhhhh?!" A barrier of putrid pepper stench blocked Mammone's path!

And...

"C'mon, Dumbante! Don't mess this up! ...*Spara la magia per mirare... Salire! And! Salire!*"

"One more for good measure! ...*Spara la magia per mirare... Salire!*"

With support spells from Wise and Medhi, Amante's attack was raised through the roof...

And she came rocketing through the hologram memories.

"Maybe *we* can use the power of family bonds, too!"

She reached out, remembering the first time she'd held Hahako's hand—her mother's hand.

Two sabers appeared, linked at the hilts by an umbilical cord–like ribbon.

The parent blade, Genitore—and the child blade, Figlio.

Amante grabbed Figlio's hilt and landed in front of Dark God Mammone.

"Wha? Wait, wait...?!"

"Dark God Mammone, I'm here to take her back! I don't have to explain *who*!"

She thrust the blade forward, and the shock wave pierced Dark God Mammone's body.

Hahako was lying at the center of the deactivated magic circle.

The blurring that had signaled her destruction had stopped, but she had yet to awaken.

"Damn it! Healing magic isn't helping, recovery items don't work, what else is there? ...Mom, any ideas? You're our last hope!"

"Let me see…having all that spoiling energy sucked out of her, and being so upset about it, would have worn her maternal side out. Ma-kun, can you give me a hand? There's something I'd like to try."

Santa Mamako took Hahako's hand in her right hand and, with her left hand, thumped her own shoulder. Did she want Masato to thump her shoulder? "I'm lost, but fine…" He began lightly thumping her shoulder, a time-honored massage technique to ease a parent's weary bones.

The close-knit family skill Filial Piety activated!

Whatever the effects of the shoulder message might be, parents were always overjoyed when children did something for them. What could be better?

The joy Santa Mamako felt went through her other hand, flowing into Hahako.

"If we can refuel her mother's feelings, I'm sure she'll get better."

"No, wait, there's no way this'll—"

"Urp…oh my? I feel so happy all of a sudden. What's happening?"

"She woke up!"

Hahako's eyes had opened. Her complexion looked good. "I barely even did anything…" Moms were pushovers, but it was best not to say that out loud.

Santa Mamako helped Hahako sit up. She looked around and saw Masato close at hand.

And right behind him, the three Kings. They were all staring at Hahako, clearly worried, but the instant their eyes met, they hastily turned away. They then slowly looked back and quickly looked away again.

"I don't remember much after Mone threw her arms around me… but they seem extra-awkward. Did something happen?"

"That's putting it lightly. But…maybe it's not for me to explain."

"We can only push them so far. The rest is up to them. As it should be."

"Yes…then I'll refrain from gathering data and reconstructing my memories. And wait for them to speak instead."

Hahako looked happy. Regardless of how they were currently acting toward her, she'd avoided destruction and was able to gaze upon them again—and that was all she needed.

It was a very maternal look, and Masato breathed a sigh of relief.

"You look after Hahako, Mom. I'll go check on the others."

"Yes, please do."

Masato got up and headed toward the edge of the magic circle.

The girls were standing in a circle—Wise and Medhi with weapons raised, and Porta with a tight grip on a bottle of green pepper perfume.

At the center of the circle was Dark God Mammone, eyes rolled back in her head, sprawled on her back like a dead frog. It was extremely undignified.

"How's it going here?" asked Masato.

"No change. She ain't moving," said Wise.

"She is breathing, so we can safely say she's alive, but…"

"If she wakes up, she might still be crazy! I'm very worried!"

"Hopefully she'll be back to the old Mone, but she's still in Dark God form, so…I guess if worst comes to worst, we can make a cage out of green peppers and carry her out in that…mm? Yo?!"

Dark God Mammone's body had suddenly started floating upward. Everyone braced themselves. Once she was upright, she released a blinding light.

The horn on her head vanished. The Dark God's equipment faded away. She was back in Mone's original costume.

She still had wings, but they'd switched from bat to bird, and were now gold.

And when her eyes opened, they shone with a golden light.

"Whoa! Mone's all sparkly!"

"What the… This isn't, like, a second form, is it? Round two?"

"Don't worry. I'm not looking for a fight. You defeated me, and I've thrown aside my past as a Dark God. I'm born anew. Now, I am an angel. The Angel of Spoiling, Spoiel."

"An…angel?! Is she being serious right now?!"

"If she's making this up, she'll have to bear the shame for the rest of her life. So, Mone, have you actually ascended?!"

"…Erk…"

Wise and Medhi shuddered, then added some unnecessary commentary of their own. The angel's smile abruptly grew very shifty, and then she started crying.

"*Hic*...Masatoooo! Wise and Medhi are sooo mean! Wahhh!"

"Yikes!"

Angel Mone had thrown her arms around Masato and was rubbing against his cheek. How spoiled. She looked different but was definitely acting just like the old Mone.

"Uh, Mone...I take it you're back to your old self, then?"

"Yep, it's me! Actually, it was me the whole time I was a Dark God. I just got a bit carried away! I knew if you defeated me, I'd become an angel, so I pretended to be someone else in the hopes that this would let me get away with it all. I'm a tricky li'l NPC! Wahhh!"

"Um, you totally just admitted to everything. But I respect the honesty, at least!"

"Regardless, we can't let you get off scot-free," Medhi said. "Prepare the punishment!"

She snapped her fingers, and Porta held out the green pepper perfume.

"Eeeeeep?! Don't, don't! No more peppers! Masato, please! Forgive me! I'm sorry for all the problems I caused!"

"Mm...sure, you put us through the wringer, but you caused problems for the whole world. I'm afraid—"

"You're kidding! I'm begging you! I'll do anything you want!"

"Oh-ho? *Anything?*" *Smirk.*

"Er...? W-well, by 'anything,' I mean... What are you thinking of making me do? It wouldn't be anything...lecherous, would it?"

Angel Mone swiftly backed away, but Masato's leer was in hot pursuit!

"Masatooo! This is no way to treat me!"

"You stole the gold star and then lost it. This is your fault. If we don't want the Christmas event ending prematurely, you've got to act as a decoration!"

"Blegh."

"I wanna hear a 'Yes, sir!' from you! We'll bring you some food and drink once the party gets started, so just hang in there awhile."

"Yes, siiiir."

He was tying Angel Mone to the top of the giant Christmas tree, her golden wings folded in the shape of a star.

It was still Christmas Eve.

The Motherest Mountains were all lit up. The transformed trees were glowing brightly.

Red, green, yellow—lights of all colors reflecting on the falling powder snow.

They placed Mammone's stolen presents beneath these trees, where they wouldn't be buried in snow or soaked through. Once that was done, Masato stretched, rubbing his stiff shoulders.

"That's the last of 'em! …Man, there's a lot."

As far as the eye could see, every tree had presents piled under it.

Christmas presents drawn from across the world, all gathered here. It was quite a sight.

Shiraaase and Dark-Mom Deathmother approached with hot cocoa.

"You defeated the Dark God and recovered the presents. Well done. Most impressive."

"Good work, Masato. You've earned yourself a break."

"Thanks."

He took a sip. Perfectly sweetened. Warmed his body through.

"A bit late for hot choco*late*, perhaps. Heh-heh-heh." Shiraaase snickered.

"Please, no puns now; this is a serious conversation."

"You wish to discuss the redistribution plan?"

"Exactly."

The wind on their backs was not nearly as chilly as their stares, but Masato stood his ground.

"It's progressing smoothly. Deathmother and Porta's Appraise skills are identifying the presents' owners, and they're being sorted by destination."

"Now we just have to transport them…but the toy shop was a limited-time function, and it already expired, so that transport option is unavailable. The only option left is to transport them ourselves. Which means…"

"…Those, huh?"

They all turned to look at the two giant sleighs standing at the base of the giant Christmas tree. They had reindeer already attached.

"Honestly, I feel like transport magic would be faster…"

"Aesthetic is important. It *is* Christmas Eve."

"And the ones delivering the presents are, obviously—"

"Mommy Santas!" Mamako said, as if she'd been wearing that outfit all night for just this moment.

As she came up to stand next to Masato, he glanced over the outfit once more and shook his head.

"Okay, okay, we'll go with that. I wish it showed a little less skin, and the name needs work, but it's all…acceptable."

"Oh, I'm so happy! Ma-kun gave me a compliment! Tee-hee."

"What's this? He was so opposed to it at first—perhaps he has grown up after all. How disappointing."

"I've grown up so much, I'm not even fazed by your teasing, Shiraaase. Ha-ha-ha."

"Really? Hmm…" Dark-Mom Deathmother gave him a quick once-over, clearly in producer mode.

But before she could say anything else…

"Right, everyone. We're ready to help!"

More delivery workers. Wise, Medhi, and Porta had all emerged from behind the curtains they'd set up in the party area.

They were all wearing Santa outfits. Now they had a cheeky Santa, a clean-cut one, and a super-energetic Santa. Three very different types of Santa girl.

"Yo, Wise, you're supposed to be a sled. Take this seriously."

"Yeah, yeah, I figured you'd say that. Speak for yourself."

"I was disappointed, too, but…if you consider how the children receiving the presents feel, these outfits are much more appropriate."

"Kids might wake up and see us! I like being Santa!"

"Good point. Fair enough. Wise, I'll allow you to be a Santa."

"Um, I wasn't seeking your permission! Who do you think you are?"

"More important—oh, my adorable Santa daughter! Let your mother gaze upon that out— ...Wait."

Deathmother stopped herself mid-dote-pounce.

The party room curtain had been drawn back completely, and Hahako emerged, dressed exactly like Mamako. And behind her were the Libere Kings.

Amante's outfit was tiger-striped. Sorella's had bones on it. Fratello's a shark. But each of them was wearing a Santa suit Dark-Mom Deathmother had prepared for them.

None of them were smiling.

"We just have to deliver these presents, right? Let's get started."

They checked over the map they'd been given, piled presents on the giant magic tome, and flew off.

Santa Hahako wordlessly watched them go.

"...They're still doing that, huh?" Masato said, shaking his head.

"Yep. Whole time we were changing. All grumpy. Refusing to talk. Not a word to Hahako."

"They saved Hahako. They changed into the costumes Deathmother made them. They've clearly changed. I don't doubt that, but—"

"Urgh, it's so frustrating! Why can't they just let it out? That's what I do!"

Santa Porta turned to give her mommy a hug. Dark-Mom Deathmother threw her arms wide to hug her back! "Oops, excuse me." Shiraaase swooped in and got in the way.

A fierce battle ensued, but the rest of them ignored it.

"The rest is up to them. They've gotta process their own feelings somehow."

"Yep. That's what we decided to let them do. Right, so we'd better get—"

"These presents delivered! Yay!"

"Mm. Yep. Look, I've accepted a lot about you, Mom, but jumping all over my heroic speeches every time still rankles."

Santa Mommy, the Santa girls, and one dude set out…!

"Oh, first, Masato, you get changed."

"I got you an outfit, too."

"Ooh, really? What kind?"

Sleigh One was the Santa Mamako team: Santa Wise, Santa Medhi, and Santa Porta.

"…Why…?"

And Snowman Masato. In a snowman costume.

Sleigh Two was Santa Hahako. Her intended backup had flown off, so Shiraaase and Dark-Mom Deathmother were pinch-hitting. They, too, had become Mommy Santas and were helping distribute presents.

"Why…? Why a snowman…? Can't we have *one* male Santa?"

"Quit moping around! Smile! We're delivering dreams, so you gotta look the part."

"Ma-kun, girls, are you ready? Let's go!"

Santa Mamako took the reins, bells rang, and the reindeer started running. Their hooves kicked the snow, then the frigid air, and they were off into the skies above.

"Whoa! We're flying! I'm flying!"

"We're going really fast, but it doesn't feel cold. Thanks to the heating effects of the mom skill A Mother's Warmth, this is quite comfortable."

"Right, everyone, we'll be meet up later. Hi ho, Silver!" *Ding-a-ling-ling!*

"Shiraaase?! That reference is really outdated and—drive safelyyyyyyy!"

"Deathmother, do be careful. You would not survive a fall from this height."

Stacked high with presents, the other sleigh went off in a peal of laughter, a shrill scream trailing behind. One sleigh went southwest, the other southeast. Headed for the towns and villages of the world.

The children were sleeping, all tucked their beds, their stockings hung with care.

And in the next room, their parents weren't sleeping, unsettled by the loss of the presents.

In one house in the capital of Catharn...

"We'll just have to get a different present...no, that won't work. The shops are closed, we can't buy anything now...we have nothing for my child...what can I do?"

One mother was sitting at an open window, staring up at the sky.

"If there is a Santa Claus out there, please, bring my child a present! I'm begging you!"

Her words were lost in the frigid wind.

She was all grown up. She knew there was no Santa Claus. She was grasping at straws, letting the words flow unbidden. Feeling sorry for herself, she got up to close the window.

But then...

"...Oh my... What's this?"

She heard the faint jingle of bells coming her way. From outside. Not believing her ears, she leaned out the window.

A sleigh pulled by reindeer was flying across the sky.

And on the sleigh was a mountain of presents, and several Santas! And also a snowman.

"Huh? But you're...Mamako!"

"Shh! Don't wake the children. Quietly!"

Mommy Santa turned to the back of the sleigh, and the snowman and Santa girls scurried around. "This house is..." "Oh, that one!" She picked up a box with a blue ribbon, for a boy.

The Mommy Santa passed the present to the mother.

"It's this one, right?"

"Yes, it is! That's it! The present I bought for... No, that's not right. This...this is a present from Santa Claus!"

"Tee-hee. That's right. You can proudly tell him it's from Santa."

The Mommy Santa winked, and the bells jingled. The reindeer pulled out, and the sleigh flew away, to the next delivery point.

Meanwhile, in a different town...

"Why must we deliver things like this? What is the goal here? Revenge for me driving too fast?"

"Merely following tradition. Hahako, set me down. Gently."

"Very well. Take care!"

The sleigh stopped in midair, and a Mommy Santa climbed out, clutching a present. White hands lowered her down the chimney below.

A few minutes later, they heard voices coming up the chimney. "I can infooorm you I have returned your present!" "Th-thanks...?" After a brief exchange, she tugged on the white hands, signally the successful present delivery.

"Looks like it went well. Hahako, pull her up! As hard as you can."

"As hard as I can? Got it. Here we go!"

She yanked, and there was a thud, followed by a painful scraping sound.

A Christmas-decorated coffin emerged from the chimney.

"Hmm. I, for one, feel much better."

"Deathmother...you certainly have a charming personality."

The Mommy Santas' infighting was growing worse, but the second sleigh set off on its course once more.

And in a town on the coast...

"Was that the last house here?"

"It waaaas. There's no more preseeeents."

"Mm. All done."

Three Santa girls on a giant magic tome flew off along the coast.

The town was silent on the holy night. Only the lights strung along the outside walls of the giant tower were busily flashing away.

"...This is where our Rebellion started."

"Yeah, I remembeeeeeer. If you conquer the tower dungeeeeeon, it'll grant you any wiiiish. A certain someone ran off alooooone and totally blew iiiiit."

"Then they called us, cryin' and beggin' for help."

"I have no memory of *that*. Humph."

They looked up at the tower, like it was an old memory.

The tome was flying slower. It soon came to a stop.

Bathed in the tower's lights, for a while, no one spoke.

"I thiiiiink I've made up my miiind."

"Mm. I'm all fired up."

They turned to the last member.

"…It'll mean refuting and abandoning everything we've ever believed. You're sure?"

"Ooooh, so that's what you're worried aboooout? How seriouuuus. But I don't think it's really refuuuuting or abaaandoning anything."

"Mm. Everyone feels like we do sometimes. Every kid out there goes through it. Parents just accept it. Sonny said so."

"…Yeah, I know he did. Argh. After all we've been through, I hate that it's Masato Oosuki's words that got through to me, but…"

She looked up at her point of origin, scowling as fierce as any tiger.

"I am one of the three Four Heavenly Kings of the Libere Rebellion, she who rebels against mothers, Anti-Mom Amante!"

Her voice rang out.

The others were taken aback by this, but then they smiled.

"And I'm one of the Four Heavenly Kings of the Libere Rebeeeellion, she who scorns all mothers, Scorn-Mom Sorellaaaaa!"

The final vowel lingered.

And the last of them turned her dazed eyes to the sky above.

"I'm one of the Four Heavenly Kings of the Libere Rebellion, the one who threatens the power of mothers, Frighten-Mom Fratello."

*　　*　　*

"We'll leave our titles and Rebellion names here. Come on. We've got presents to deliver."

Three Santa girls headed off to the edge of the world, looking quite reinvigorated.

Time had passed. It was now late at night.

Masato's party had finished distributing their presents and had regrouped at the base of the giant fir tree (where Angel Mone was dozing off).

They'd plopped themselves down together on the couches in the party area and ceased to move—too tired even to reach for the hot milk Mamako had brought them.

"You must be exhausted, Ma-kun. Can I sit next to you?"

"Go ahead. You're probably just as tired, Mom. We managed to get everything delivered, but it sure took a while. You on the right, what time is it?"

"I dunno. Ask the one to the right of me. All I know is I'm sleepy. *Yawn...*"

"Wise, that's so undig—*yawn*—o-oh my, what's come over me?"

"Pfft, even you can't stop yourself yawning, Medhi. Oh, Mamako, too."

"Oh dear, you saw that? Tee-hee. It's been a very busy day. Just look at Porta!"

The older kids had changed back to their normal gear, but Porta was still a Santa girl. She'd been far too sleepy to change, diving headfirst onto a two-seater couch. Her head rested on Dark-Mom Deathmother's lap.

If the kids were tired, the mothers were, too. Shiraaase had her head down on the banquet table. Her usual hard-to-place expression was gone, her eyes now struggling to focus.

"Shiraaase, that's giving you a terrifying squint..."

"The fatigue caught up with me...but don't be alarmed... Before I pass out, I *will* think of a way to get Hotta back...maybe I'll viciously wake Porta up or..." *Staaare.*

"Not happening! I will protect her precious sleeping face!" *Hiss.*

"Mmph...Mommy's voice... Whoa, did I fall asleep?!"

"Oh no, did I wake you?!"

"You shouted so loud, you woke her yourself... Mm, not my problem."

Masato wanted to just sink into the couch and sleep right here, but he forced himself to sit up. He couldn't sleep yet.

The Libere Kings weren't back yet.

Hahako was standing out on the snow, waiting for them. There was snow piling up on her head and shoulders, and she was holding an armful of presents, watching the sky.

What are they doing? They are *planning to come back...right?*

He had to have faith.

They'd been doing their best to brush aside concerns and maintain a jovial atmosphere, but they were running out of steam. It was starting to get awfully quiet.

No one was saying anything.

The log on the fire crackled.

Snow fell.

Then Hahako let out a little gasp. "Oh..."

A giant magic tome was approaching through the falling snow.

"Augh, we finally made iiiiit! That took so loooong!"

"It's Amante's fault. If we hadn't taken that detour, we woulda been back ages ago."

"I don't need to explain this again, but we had no choice! We had to get ready! Gimme a break!"

All three had returned, wailing, scolding, and yelling explanations, their moods having taken a complete one-eighty.

Masato was relieved and took a gulp of...lukewarm milk.

"They made us worry for nothing... I'm gonna go yell at 'em."

"Wait, Ma-kun."

When he tried to get up, Mamako grabbed his arm. She smiled gently and shook her head.

He glanced to his right. "You can't interfere *now*." "Read the room."

Wise and Medhi chuckled and went back to pretending they were asleep.

Porta really *was* asleep, and Shiraaase and Dark-Mom Deathmother had their eyes closed and their ears perked.

"...Sorry. Guess heroes can't solve everything."

Masato resisted Mamako's efforts to pull him closer to her, and he let his head rest against the couch, closing his eyes.

Amante, Sorella, and Fratello hopped off the magic tome and lined up in front of Hahako.

Hahako wasn't sure what to say at first. Then she finally made up her mind.

"Welcome home," she said.

"...We're back."

"We're baaaack!"

"Mm. Good to be back."

The greetings were pretty average...

...But that alone was enough to make tears well up in Hahako's eyes. She fought them back then took a step toward the girls.

"You must be tired. The three of you worked very hard, didn't you?"

"Not really. We can handle this much work, no problem."

"Oh, really? That is impressive. Weren't you cold?"

"We're fiiiine. These clothes are waaaarm."

"I'm glad to hear it. But um...aren't you tired at all?"

"Mm. Not especially. Like Amante said, we're good."

"G-good...I asked the same thing twice, didn't I?"

The Kings didn't smile or anything, but they were responding normally.

Interpreting that as a positive sign, Hahako took another step closer.

But she seemed at a loss as to what to do next. She opened her mouth, but no words came.

Amante sighed. She glanced at the bundle in Hahako's arms.

"What's that?"

"Hm? Oh, these are your Christmas presents. I don't know if you'll like them, but—"

"Ohhh! I wonder what's insiiiide? Can we open themmm?"

"Y-yes, of course."

Looking nervous, Hahako held out the bundle. Amante took it from her and opened it carefully.

Inside was an album.

They flipped open the cover. It started with pictures of Hahako holding the Heavenly Kings as babies, then with them at age three, then with them as ten-year-olds…and finally pictures from when they'd been active with the Libere Rebellion. Even photos of them fighting Masato's party and Hahako.

"I dunno how ya took some of these…"

"This is called a Mother-Child Album. It automatically captures photos of particular individuals and adds them to an album. It's a rare item that was the grand prize in the Matriarchal Arts Tournament, so Mamako had one, and I copied it…"

"And thiiiis is our present?"

"Y-yes, it is. I thought we needed…um…family memories. They're stored in here, so we can share them… I thought that might be… lovely."

"I see. Then…"

Amante snapped the album shut and shoved it toward Hahako.

"Um… O-oh, I see. You don't like it… I'm sorry…"

"No, that's not it. This is something a mother ought to have. Not her kids. You should hold on to it."

"Oh…I understand. It's a mother's item, so I should…… Hm?"

Hahako looked up at them, stunned.

They all avoided her eyes, turning to Dark-Mom Deathmother.

"Master…no, Saori Hotta! Listen up! We don't hate you anymore!"

"We have historyyyy, but you gave us more than you tooook. Like this Christmas eveeeent."

"We're only here today 'cause y'all made use of us. So we're good on that. Heck, maybe even grateful."

"However! We don't consider you our birth mother. We only need one mom!"

Dark-Mom Deathmother's eyes went wide, then she bit her lip and hung her head. She nodded several times. Apologetically. Gratefully.

And then the girls turned back toward Hahako.

"Hahako, we've got a present for you. Will you accept it?"

Amante, Fratello, and Sorella all reached into their pockets.

Then they took out some ribbons and wrapped them around themselves, tying a bow.

There.

Hahako simply stared wide-eyed at them.

"H-hey! Get the picture?! We're giving you the gift of children! Don't make me explain—"

An instant later, the three girls were wrapped in their mother's embrace. Pressed up against the soft warmth of their mother's chest, no further explanation was necessary.

Masato's party opened their eyes just wide enough to see, then closed them again.

It was Christmas Eve—possibly late enough to be Christmas already, but that no longer mattered.

They were all going to have the sweetest dreams.

A Christmas Memory

Mamako

Last is Mommy's memories!

No talking about our family Christmases. I'm worried the pain will kill me.

Masato

Mamako

Oh, such a shame. Then what about something from when Mommy was a child? Like the first time I met the real Santa!

Um, you met the real one? Like, he actually exists?!

Wise

Medhi

If Mamako says so, I'm sure he does.

I always believed in Santa! I knew he was real!

Porta

Masato

No, no, that's ridiculous... Wait... is that a sleigh flying this way?!

MERRY CHRISTMAS, MAMAKO OOSUKI

Epilogue

Christmas morning.

Catharn was blanketed in white, and children's squeals rang out from homes all over. They'd woken up to find presents by their pillows!

From whom? "Why, Santa, of course!" their parents answered with a smile, and the children's eyes went as wide as dinner plates.

In the merchant town of Yomamaburg, no snow fell. Instead, there was a fluttering rain of silver chips. The casino's Christmas display was very popular.

The manager smiled warmly as parents and children alike flocked to the casino interior, hoping odds were spoiled in their favor. (The odds of winning on each game…remained unchanged.)

Meema had plenty of snow, and the guards, dressed as Santas, were starting the Christmas parade. Decorated trees had been set up outside the Matriarchal Arts Tournament venue, and the parade started there, went down the main road, and then spread out through the streets. The guards wound through every road in town, handing out cookies to all the nice children…

But the white-bearded guards were swarmed by innocent beastkin kids, who seemed liable not only to snatch presents but to rip their arms off, too. The beastkin mothers swooped in to stop them, looking pale.

In the seaside town of Thermo, the celebrations took on a distinctly aquatic flair.

With the heavily decorated tower dungeon watching over them, parents changed into swimsuits, day-care workers tied Christmas-themed loincloths tight, and all plunged into the frigid ocean. They collected presents from the depths, bringing them up to the children on the shore.

The festival celebrated the bounty of the sea and the growth of the children. Local customs varied, okay?

And...

At the far end of the world, at the base of the Motherest Mountains...

The giant Christmas tree bedecked with Angel Mone gave off the most brilliant light in all the world.

"Masatooo! Heyyyy! How long do I have to stay up here?"

"Just a little longer! The event will automatically wrap up just after noon! Leene said she'll spoil you rotten as soon as you finish making up for all your bad deeds."

"Mommy said that?! Hooray! That will be the best! I'm so much more motivated now!"

With the spoiled angel watching over them, the Christmas party began in earnest.

The banquet table in the party venue was laden with all kinds of food. Painstakingly crafted hors d'oeuvres, roasted chicken, Christmas cakes, and more. The spread was a bit heavy for so early in the day—well, only the weak-stomached grown-ups thought that. The children were delighted.

There was enough food for twelve.

Currently at the venue were Masato, Mamako, Wise, Medhi, Porta, Dark-Mom Deathmother, and Shiraaase. Also technically Angel Mone. Only eight people.

They were holding off the start of the feast.

Shiraaase tried to steal a bite, but Dark-Mom Deathmother slapped her hand away.

Shiraaase looked around at everyone present, then said, "Well, to while away the time, I suppose we could have the children open the presents they've been dying to receive."

""""""Yeah!""""""

The kids gathered on the couches, presents from their mothers in hand. Their mothers smiled as the unwrapping ceremony began.

"Who's first?"

"An excellent question. Wise should definitely go last, since she's bound to be the punchline," said Medhi.

"The punchline?! Ugh, you're probably right… It's painfully obvious by now…"

"Then can I open mine? I'm too excited to wait!"

Porta was already pulling on the pink ribbon.

Inside was a key, decorated with Christmas colors.

But what was it a key to? Puzzled, Porta looked at Dark-Mom Death-mother, who just smiled. In which case…

"I'll appraise it! Hnggg…this is a key that makes something appear! I think it's better to use it somewhere with lots of room! I'm gonna go do just that!"

Porta dashed out onto the snowfield, stuck the key into thin air, and turned it.

A treasure chest appeared in front of her, one so big not only Porta but even Masato could probably fit inside. The lid popped open.

Inside the chest were stuffed animals, clothes, shoes, everything a girl could ever want.

"Whoa! There's so much! …M-Mommy! Can I really have so many presents?!"

"Of course! Because I was a fool, I hadn't given you any Christmas presents in such a long time. So I thought I'd give you enough to make up for it!"

"Mommy…I'm so happy! Mommy!"

"My beloved daughter!"

Porta and her mother threw their arms around each other, tears trailing in their wakes. The scene was incredibly heartwarming.

"You're just too cute! Hff, hff!"

"M-Mommy?"

Deathmother's head had overheated a bit, and her glasses had fogged up. Sauna-tastic!

Moving right along…

"I'll go next… Oh? This is…"

Medhi had unraveled an elegant blue ribbon and found a delicately crocheted headband and a message card.

To my beloved daughter. So that your heart and mind stay beautiful, I'm sending you equipment with a sedative effect.

The letters were slightly uneven, but her handwriting had certainly improved a lot.

"Mother... A sedative effect...? Heh-heh-heh...thank you kindly."

Rumble.

"Medhi! Equip that now! You need it ASAP!"

"And that's not even a game world item, right? It's just a pricey-looking accessory!"

"Now that you mention it, yes... Honestly, Mother. You and your little jokes."

Medhi put on the headband and smiled happily. A mother's love and a little light teasing did a good job calming any child's heart.

"You fell right for Medhimama's plan. Mothers sure know their stuff. Okay, then..."

"Wait, Masato. I'm next. Better to be disappointed early. Gives me time to recover."

"Damn, that's sad."

It was Wise's turn. She took her present, said a prayer, gathered her mental fortitude, preparing herself for anything, and ripped off the red plastic tape and newspaper.

Her hands shaking, she removed the lid, whispering, "Please, God!"

It was empty.

"Argh...that idiot! You've gotta be kidding me!"

"Kazuno, the Queen of the Night...you never disappoint. Never let your daughter have a moment's... Oh, wait, Wise, look again."

"I already saw! It's empty! Arghhhhh!"

"No, on the lid."

"......Huh?"

She'd almost crushed the lid in anger, but taped to the inside was a pair of earrings with a brand-name logo.

There was also a note in ballpoint pen.

I sneaked into your room and saw your magazine. You had circled a bunch of things, but these were the cheapest.

"Wha…who let her in my room? Geez."

"That's the only comment you have?"

"You know you're happy. Heh-heh-heh." Medhi giggled.

"Oh, shut up. Just when you least expect it…ugh."

Wise was muttering under her breath, but when she looked down at the earrings in her hand, she couldn't stop herself from smiling.

Now then.

"Last is Ma-kun! I do hope it makes you happy."

Mamako smoothly found a seat next to him and watched closely as he opened the present. "I didn't know you could draw…," he said. There was a cartoony illustration of him on the long, slim package. Inside was…

A rather fancy necktie.

"A tie? Why a tie? I mean, I don't dislike it, but…it's very unexpected."

"I just thought you might be needing one soon. Well?"

"That is a surprise. Does she have ESP?" *Stare.*

"You can't underestimate Mamako for a second." *Stare.*

"Yikes, what's going on here?"

Shiraaase and Dark-Mom Deathmother had popped up behind them, looking over his shoulders. Muttering to each other and staring at the necktie with great interest. He was totally lost.

"A-anyway, Mom, thanks. If I have a chance to wear it, I definitely will."

"You're welcome, Ma-kun. I'd be delighted to see it on you."

"So that wraps up present time, but…oh dear."

Shiraaase stared out at the snowfield, casually swiping a piece of fried chicken.

Before she could grab another, everyone stopped her—and then they all looked in the same direction.

Still no sign of Hahako.

"...If they're being all distant now, we can't just let that happen," Masato muttered.

Everyone nodded.

Shiraaase offered to remain behind, and Dark-Mom Deathmother volunteered instead, in order to prevent her from eating everything.

The rest of them hopped onto a sleigh, going back the way they'd come. They traveled across the brutally cold snow and through the door to the transfer point on the plateau near the Catharn capital.

They were so high up, it was hard not to flinch, but they looked out at the world...and saw four people leaving the capital.

"Hngg...that...is definitely them! Hahako's family!"

"Then let's stop them with a few attack spells!" *Grin.*

"They deserve a punishment! ...*Spara la magia...*"

"Stop that."

They ran down the stairs, giving chase.

When they finally caught up with them, Hahako turned around, looking blissfully happy.

Sorella and Fratello turned toward them, also smiling, bleary and dazed eyes, respectively, looking quite happy.

Amante didn't turn around.

"...Sheesh, nobody asked you to see us off."

"We're not here to see you off. We're here to make sure you take part in the Christmas party."

"Riiiight...we were going to do thaaat..."

"But it ain't good to get too chummy. We've got other fish to fry."

"I'm so sorry, these children said they wanted to go on an adventure as a family. I said we could still do that after breakfast at the party, but..."

"No worries. We're not hungry."

Her stomach growled. Everyone turned and looked at Amante. "You're hearing things!" she said, punching her own stomach to shut it up.

Recovering, Amante wheeled around. Looking much more at peace than she ever had before.

"We've at last accepted her as our mother. So you win the final battle. But we won't lose next time!"

"Do you know what 'final' means? Whatever... What's next, then?"

"Do I have to explain everything? Sheesh. Obviously, this battle!"

Amante hooked her arm in Hahako's. Fratello stepped up on Hahako's left, holding her hand. Sorella went around back, hugging her.

Hahako smiled like she had never been happier, while the three sisters grinned like this was a challenge.

"Ohhh, right. The happy family battle," said Wise.

"Well, we can't lose that," said Medhi.

"Exactly! I won't ever lose that fight!" squealed Porta. "Masato!"

"...Sure."

It was still a little embarrassing. But only a little. The heroic son was largely over that.

Masato put his arm around Mamako's shoulder, puffing up his chest. """"Ohhh...."""" His party gawked, but his confident expression never wavered.

"Oh my! Ma-kun! Mommy's too happy! I don't know what's going to happen! Tee-hee!"

"Just be glad your son's grown up. See, Amante? You've got no chance of winning here. But have a good time on your family adventure."

"You may be able to lord it over us now, but just you wait! We'll become a family even stronger than yours! Later."

Former enemies, now turned rivals.

The two parties stared at each other for a long moment.

"Yeah, later."

"Yes, some other day..." *Growlllllll...*

Amante turned so red, she looked ready to explode, but Mamako took her hand.

"Tee-hee. The time for family adventures is *after* breakfast."

"O-okay, fine! You have to listen to advice from moms! We're good kids now!"

And with those words, the tale of those who rebel against mothers came to an end.

Meanwhile, by the giant Christmas tree...

Shiraaase was forced to kneel in the snow as punishment for repeated snacking violations.

As she watched the snow fall, she muttered, "The Oosukis have earned the right to challenge him. It's time."

"Yes, as we head toward the official launch, the final beta test...will soon begin."

Dark-Mom Deathmother was sitting on the couch in the party venue, staring down at her tablet, her steely producer's gaze on.

On the screen was a design document labeled:

ADVENT OF THE DEMON LORD

Afterword

Hello, everyone! This is Inaka.

Here we are in Volume 9! My goal was secretly to reach ten volumes, so we're one step away! I'm grateful for all your support.

The stars this time were the three Four Kings and Hahako. And of course, moms. The long Libere Rebellion arc that started with Amante's first appearance has finally wound to a close. I hope you enjoyed it.

Iida Pochi., my editor K, everyone in editorial and publishing, and all the retail staff have been of invaluable assistance once again. I'd like to take this space to thank them.

About the anime version of *Mom*...

I was genuinely astonished that it was actually broadcast. That alone was far too much for me, and I was floating on air for days on end.

Thank you to everyone involved in production and the broadcast itself.

Spira Spica, thank you for the lovely opening song. "Iyayo Iyayo Mo Suki no Uchi" is an upbeat number you and your mother can dance to together. On sale now! Also celebrating a year since their major label debut!

The anime led to all kinds of events, to online radio shows filled with lively personalities, to all kinds of merchandise, to a special in *Dragon Magazine*, to a special comic done by Meicha (who does the manga version of this series), to so many magazine and news articles... I was thrilled and excited by it all. Given the limited space in this afterword, I'm sadly unable to thank them all by name.

By the way…

I secretly went to watch a "Hero event," where people lie down on Mamako's lap pillows to watch the anime on the streets of Akihabara. It sure was a sight.

There were way more people than I'd expected, and I didn't want to keep anyone else waiting their turn, so I elected not to be a Hero. Even though I reeeeally wanted to.

I saw some foreign tourists stop to take a bunch of pictures of the lap pillow event, and that really stuck with me. Watching anime on your mother's lap may soon become the worldwide standard… That's a potential future anyway.

By the time this volume reaches you, the anime will be wrapping up. Only the last episode will remain! (Depending on your region and broadcast stations.)

I've had more than enough happiness for one lifetime, and yearning for anything more would be far too great an indulgence, clearly asking for trouble, but…well, even as I wrap that up, I do still have ambitions.

Let us hope that more of my dreams come true. I hope I will receive even more support from all of you. Thank you in advance.

Lastly, I received a text from my mother.

"Glad the wind's blowing your way. Don't get a big head, though."

I intend to carve these words into my heart.

Midsummer 2019, Dachima Inaka